Malice
Murder

Malice Murder

Robert Coburn

A Jack Hunter Mystery

ABSOLUTELY AMAZING eBOOKS

ABSOLUTELY AMAZING eBOOKS

Published by Whiz Bang LLC, 926 Truman Avenue, Key West, Florida 33040, USA.

For information contact:
Publisher@AbsolutelyAmazingEbooks.com

ISBN-13: 978-1945772191 (Absolutely Amazing Ebooks)
ISBN-10: 1945772190

To Kate and those she helps.

Other Books by Robert Coburn

A Loose Knot

A Deadly Deception

The Pink Gun

Little Boxes

Bad Tidings

An Evil Number

Malice
Murder

Chapter 1

One more door until freedom. He could see his lawyer waiting for him on the other side through the window. He looked bored. Too bad.

He sucked in. The cheap suit didn't fit any better now than it had at his trial. Then it'd hung loosely. Today it was so tight he could hardly button the pants, the jacket threatening to split down the back at any minute. He'd bulked up considerably with the yard weights. It was incredible that the lawyer had brought along the same damn suit. Probably had a whole closet full of them. Out-of-style threads for out-of-luck chumps. But why couldn't he have at least picked one in his size?

He noticed the guard standing by the door smirking. He could only imagine how ridiculous he looked. There was no mirror in the room.

Should he bother with the tie? He'd like to wrap it around the guard's neck and pull until the sucker choked. He decided to stuff it in the jacket pocket.

~~~

Inmate C82735 had served three years of a maximum eleven-year sentence for manslaughter at Pleasant Valley State Prison in Coalinga, California. Those who'd known the victim, a prominent businesswoman in Los Angeles, had demanded he be charged with first-degree murder and then given life without even the slightest hope of ever being paroled. The district attorney had sympathized with them but in California law the evidence wouldn't have supported murder-one so he'd charged him with the next serious offense that would stick. Voluntary manslaughter.

But at trial the judge had given erroneous instructions to the jury, which eventually led to an appeal. To everyone's dismay, the conviction was overturned and, while there was the possibility of getting a retrial, the DA decided against pursuing the cause. It would've been too expensive and there was always the risk of an acquittal. He held that the prisoner had already been inside for three years and prison years are much, much longer, than outside.

~~~

He had finished dressing. His prison clothes were neatly piled on a bench. The guard, still holding the smirk, clapped a pair of cuffs on him and signaled to the officer waiting outside the room to buzz open the door.

"We'll keep a light on for you, asshole," he said.

Chapter 2

The report of a possible dead body was called in by a cab driver. The cabbie said a homeless guy had approached his taxi at a gas station on North Roosevelt and told him there was a dead man in the Blue Bayou. The dispatcher asked that the two of them wait there until the police arrived, but the homeless man hadn't stuck around. After getting a description of him from the cab driver, the cops went directly to the location. It didn't take them long to find the victim. A male possibly in his late twenties or early thirties lay sprawled on the bank, his body halfway into the water. His head bashed in.

The patrol radioed for detectives.

~~~

Blue Bayou is the name given by Key West's considerable homeless population to the mangrove-tangled thicket along a narrow cut which led in from the Gulf of Mexico. It was the oldest such encampment on the two-by-four miles of the island.

Key West, like other warmer cities across the country, had become a homeless destination. To its credit, the city had worked mightily to find a solution to the problem. A work always in progress and never getting anywhere.

~~~

"Nobody around when you got here?" Detective Earl Gleason questioned the patrol officer.

"Even the birds had gone, detective," he answered. "My partner and I got the call. Came here. Discovered the deceased. Took one look and called for detectives."

"What about the cab driver?"

"He was waiting for us at the gas station. We asked him about the person who'd reported the body but apparently the guy split before we arrived."

"Any description? Had he seen him around before?"

"Another homeless is all the cabbie could tell us. Didn't pay all that much attention to him."

"Young, old, black, white?" Gleason pressed. "Looked like he'd been homeless for a while? Have all his marbles? I'm just trying to get a better fix. Might help us find him."

"Driver wasn't all that forthcoming, detective," the officer said. "We got the best we could from him. Hopefully, he'll remember more when he talks to you."

"Okay, thanks, officer."

Gleason squatted next to the dead man for a closer look. He was lying face up with his legs on the bank and head settled ear-deep in the shallow brackish water.

He stood and walked back a couple of feet and bent down to examine the ground.

"Some blood here. Probably where he was attacked."

He placed a numbered marker by the spot and took a photo with his phone. A crime scene tech would take more pictures. And more.

"Looks like the guys from the medical examiner are coming, detective," the officer called out.

Gleason turned to see two men approaching.

"Watch where you step, fellows," Gleason warned. "There are blood stains where I placed that marker. Could be more."

"We got it, boss," one of them said. "We'll wait until your techs are through. Besides, the medical examiner's gonna be late."

Detective Rachel Powers joined him.

"I've got a couple of officers checking out some camp sites further in, sir," she reported. "Doesn't appear to be much around other than trash."

Powers had been with the Key West department for two years, starting in patrol and then recently moving to detectives. She had a master's degree in criminology and had served five years in the US Army, which included two tours of duty in Iraq. Gleason would be the lead detective in the investigation.

"One man's trash can be another man's evidence, detective," Gleason smiled.

"We've also strung yellow tape along the sidewalk, sir," she added. "The area is secured."

Gleason noticed Powers staring at the victim. It was a pretty gruesome sight. This was their first homicide together.

"You all right, Rachel?"

"First blow probably knocked him into the water," she stated, ignoring the question. "Maybe even killed him."

She made a hard swinging move that startled Gleason.

"Hit him right where that blood splatter is," she said, pointing to where Gleason stood. "Sent him reeling."

She leaned over the body

"Yeah, then he made sure he was dead with a couple more whacks. Splatter on the bank. I wonder if he was initially struck from behind. That's possible. He could've spun around before falling."

"Why is that important?" Gleason asked.

"Well, it could mean that the killer caught him by surprise, sir. Or maybe not. They could've been arguing and the guy turned his back to walk away. Big mistake for him."

"Let's search around the scene," Gleason said.

They spread out five feet apart and carefully walked the clearing where the body lay and extended back to the edge of some thick growth. Nothing caught either's attention.

"I'll have the crime techs sweep the entire bank," Gleason declared.

"Wonder why they call this Blue Bayou?" Powers said, more to herself. "Sounds like it ought to be in Louisiana. Wasn't there a song named that?"

She tried to hum the tune.

"No, that's not how it goes," she frowned. "Before my time, anyway."

Gleason gave her a look.

"Can't tell whether the killer was left- or right-handed," she said, bending down closer to the body. "Equal opportunity bludgeoner. Smashed up both sides of his head. ME will know."

"He's here," one of the men announced.

The medical examiner pushed his way out from the thicket and into the clearing.

"You don't make it easy, detective," he said, slapping at an annoying insect.

"I don't choose the locations, Dr. Hardy," Gleason said dourly. "Much traffic?"

Blake Hardy was the ME for Monroe County. His office was in Marathon.

"Easy drive," he said walking over to the body. "Looks familiar."

"You know this person, Dr. Hardy?" Powers asked.

"Can't place the face," Hardy answered with black humor, then said "Sorry" with a wry grin before going on. "I mean, there's been a few homeless deaths lately, haven't there?" He turned his attention to the body. "Looks like whoever did this one has issues for sure."

"I think you're reading too many pyscho murder mysteries, doctor. But the autopsy will tell us more."

"Ah, always one step ahead of me," Hardy joked again. "Okay if we move him out?"

"Let my guys get a few more pictures. Can't have enough photographs, you know."

Powers glanced in the direction of the Key West airport as the noise from a landing jet reversing its engines and braking on the short runway rumbled through the mangroves.

Chapter 3

Jack Hunter stood on the sidewalk looking at the little house as the taxi pulled away. At the mass of purple bougainvillea spilling over the fence. A million memories stared back.

He unlocked the front door and stepped inside.

The place felt as if he'd never left. He had phoned Jan Cox at the realtors to let her know that he was returning. She handled the rent payments for the owner, Ruth LaVere.

He took his bag into the bedroom and dumped it out on the bed. He traveled light since he kept plenty of clothes at the house. His saxophone, however, always went with him. He stashed it in a closet.

His seat mate on the redeye from Los Angeles to Atlanta had read all night. He felt a little spacey from the lack of sleep. A shower might be just the thing to put him in the right time zone. He checked the hot water, stripped down and stepped in.

~~~

"It's the second one in this general location," Gleason said. "Someone's trying to solve the homeless problem."

"Nobody around the encampment?" Halderman asked. "Witnesses or anything?"

"What do you think?" Gleason shrugged.

Lieutenant Jay Halderman headed up detectives at KWPD. Gleason and Powers were in his office.

"Detective Powers believes the victim may have known his killer," Gleason said. "Or maybe not. Personally, I don't think it matters one way or the other."

"You might want to enlighten me on that," Halderman said. "Detective Powers?"

"If the victim was hit from behind, it could have been a surprise," Powers explained. "If he'd been facing his assailant, then he might've known him. That's the only thing I was thinking, sir."

"What do you say, Earl, a drug deal gone bad?" Halderman asked Gleason. "Like what happened over by Rest Beach."

"Possibly," Gleason nodded. "Shooter did that one, not a bludgeoner. Doesn't mean it wasn't about drugs. Thing is, most homeless people don't have the money to support a heavy drug habit. By the way, I'm going to have divers search the water. See if we can find a weapon. Pipe, golf club, whatever."

"Must be something about the Blue Bayou that brings out the worse," Haldeman said. "The last victim had what? Four stab wounds and his throat cut. Little overkill there. Now this poor bastard has his brains beaten out."

"I don't believe robbery would be a motive this time, sir," Powers put in. "Like Detective Gleason said, all most homeless have is what's in their grocery store cart."

"Going back to the other victims, I'm wondering if there *is* a connection." Gleason asked. "Did either victim know the other? Could explain the brutality. Seems like a malice murder with each one."

"Malice murder?" Powers said.

"That's a homicide committed with express or implied malice," Gleason explained.

"I helped investigate a similar homicide in Iraq," Powers said.

Both men looked at her.

"Soldier hacked his buddy to death with an entrenching tool," she said. "That's a folding shovel for digging a foxhole. Makes a great weapon. Bad blood between them. The similarities in the rage involved there and the ones we're talking about are remarkable. Yeah, overkill.   Four stab wounds. Throat slashed. Then our victim today. I can see where Detective Gleason is going. Could even be a serial killer. But how did you put it, sir? Oh, yeah, a malice murder. That would certainly describe these."

"Another possibility," Gleason said. "No connection at all between them. Just a couple of dumb fucks settling an argument."

"Let's keep this possible serial killer business to ourselves for the time being, "Halderman said. How soon can we get the medical examiner's report? Like to compare them with the others."

"I'll give Blake Hardy a call," Gleason said, getting up from his chair. "Tell him what we've just been discussing. Maybe he knows someone who can run a psychological comparison of the wounds, if there is such a thing. Sometimes a little mumbo jumbo helps. Detective Powers can check out the homeless shelter. See if anyone there knows anything."

Both detectives stood to leave.

"Hold on a minute before you go, Earl, need to ask you something," Halderman said, then motioned to Powers that she was dismissed.

Gleason sat down again. Powers left the room, shutting the door after her.

"How's she doing?" Halderman asked.

"Powers? Fine, I guess. She's enthusiastic. I don't have any problems with her. Little weird. Like saying '*sir*' all the time. What's up?"

"Nothing. Just wanted some feedback. As you probably know, there has been, well, more than a little resentment over her being jumped up to detectives so quickly."

"Seems qualified to me," Gleason said. "Who's complaining?"

"Just scuttlebutt," Halderman smiled. "You know anything about her military record?"

"Not really. She was a GI Jane, that's about it."

"She served in Iraq. Decorated, too. Given the Purple Heart. Tough lady."

"Wonder why she didn't stay in the army?" Gleason questioned. "Sounds like she had a pretty good career going."

"Must've had her reasons. Got her here in a hurry anyway. Related military service can give you a pass on having to attend a law enforcement officer training school. Complete a two-week compliance course and you're good to take the Florida state exam."

Gleason gave a wolfish grin.

"I can see where that might piss off some people."

Chapter 4

Jack bicycled along Angela Street on the way to the Inedible Cafe. It was close to noon and the sun was fast wiping out any possibility of shade and leaving the pavement to radiate enough heat for a blast furnace. His t-shirt was soaked in sweat. The tires were a little soft, too, and made the going all the more difficult. A motor scooter zipped past. He thought of the little red Vespa he'd once rented.

Billy Bean had given him the bicycle long ago when he was down and out. It'd been a godsend then and just one of many examples of Billy's generosity. He'd named it Whizzer and it was all he had needed to peddle around.

The red Vespa returned to mind.

He crossed Duval Street into Bahama Village, passing another thousand memories on the way, until at last he arrived at the restaurant. Parking the bike in the alley out back, he paused for a moment before entering through the kitchen. This odd little place with its quirky characters had been a turning point that had reset his inner compass on another and better course.

The screen door banged open and Billy Bean stepped out.

"Jack! What the hell are you doing standing here in the alley? Hee, hee."

~~~

After the lunch crowd had cleared, Jack and Billy settled at a table with a pot of coffee.

"You planning to stick around for a while?" Billy asked.

"Yeah, few things I want to do. Los Angeles is okay but I need a break. Might even cut back on some of my business there."

"Uh-huh, if it was me, I'd cut back on the whole place. LA, I mean."

Jack had just told him about his run-in with the Satanist cult while he was in California. But not everything. No need to worry Billy about near misses and narrow escapes. In fact, he'd like to forget those parts himself.

"You ever been there, Billy? Out to California?"

"California's too crazy for me, hee-hee."

"Thing I always liked about it was the energy. Especially in Los Angeles. You wake up in the morning and feel like anything's possible."

"That's supposing a fellow wakes up. Sounds to me like that's not a sure bet in LA."

"I'll take you there some day," Jack smiled, hopefully putting an end to the subject.

"No rush on that, Jack. Plenty to do here. Need to think some about Stella by Starlight. Gonna have to let the chef go."

"Really?" Jack asked in surprise. "I thought he was a hand-picked wonder. What's happening?"

"He's too much of a corner cutter, hee-hee. Puts stuff on the menu he can't pull off. Gotta know your limits, Jack."

Jack could appreciate that last part in more ways than Billy knew. But on the subject of menus, the Inedible Cafe knew *its* limits. It was limited by the number of plastic replicas that would fit in a display case— eggs sunny side up, waffles, pancakes, pork chops, steaks. A three-dimensional menu. Just point and shout.

"Secret to success," Billy continued, "is not try and fix every damn dish in the world. Just do what you're good at. Know what I'm saying, Jack?"

Actually, Jack did. That was pretty good advice in many areas, he thought.

"Sous chef's got talent. Think I can bring *him* along.

Help's hard to find on this ol' island. No matter if you want somebody just to sweep the floor, hee, hee."

~~~

The homeless shelter provided a roof over your head and a helping hand to find other services.

Rachael Powers was about to come away empty-handed, however.

"Richard Kirby was murdered there earlier," she said. "According to your records, he had stayed here."

"Poor man," Dorothy Rowe sighed.

Rowe was a volunteer at the intake desk.

"And now you say there's another one? I hope he wasn't a client."

The homeless were referred to as *clients*. It provided a little dignity. Every client signed in at the shelter. No time limit was placed on how long or how often you stayed. But you could be denied a space for a number of reasons, drug trafficking or fighting being among them.

"I'm afraid it's a possibility," Powers told her. "Happened in the same general area. It might be important to learn if the victims knew each other or if anyone here remembered them."

"Well, I wish I could help but without a name there's not much I can do. Could be he was living at another shelter. If you have a picture...oh, how stupid of me!"

She bit her lip at the thought of any photograph the police might have of the murdered men.

"We're pretty sure both men had stayed here," Powers said. "Kirby had a record for selling drugs. Nothing big. Did you know about the drugs? Is that a problem in this shelter?"

"I understand it used to be," Rowe answered. "Before my time. But it's probably why Mr. Kirby stopped coming around."

"How long have you volunteered at the shelter?" Powers

13

asked.

"Three months. My husband's stationed at Boca Chica Naval Air Station. He flies F-18s. His squadron may soon be deployed."

"Well, the very best to him. Are there many volunteers like yourself here?"

Rowe thought for a moment.

"Yes, actually there're several of us. We also share working at other shelters whenever there's a need."

"Wonder if I could get a list of volunteers?"

"You'd have to check that with the manager."

"Thanks for your time, Mrs. Rowe. I may have more questions later."

"Hope you catch whoever's doing this," Rowe called after her.

"Me, too," Powers said from the doorway.

Outside, the detective took in the shelter once more. She thought about the woman inside whose husband was a pilot. And about her own husband who once was also an airman. Then she got into her car and drove to the Blue Bayou.

Yellow crime scene tape stretched across the pathway entering the shrubby thicket. She was glad she'd worn a pantsuit today as she made her way through the tangled growth, ducking beneath low hanging branches at times. Silence greeted her at the clearing. She stood quietly and looked around.

The contrast between the beauty of the setting and the horror that'd taken place there struck her. She walked slowly to the water's edge where the body had lain and squatted, placing her hand on the spot of ground. Footprints visible in the soil where the crime techs had worked. At another time, they could've been made by anyone. Fishermen. Campers. Even the homeless.

She hadn't returned there in hope of finding much. The

whole area had been thoroughly gone over by the tech team, including herself and Gleason. No, she had come to the scene of the crime for the reason so many other detectives often did. To get a feeling. Maybe a focus. Whatever.

A bird called shrilly from somewhere deep in the mangroves. She got back to her feet and left.

Chapter 5

Jack had decided on having an early dinner at Stella by Starlight. He'd dressed in a favorite Hawaiian shirt, old jeans and a pair of high-mileage running shoes.

Sidewalk traffic was light on Duval Street. Although the sun had bowed out to a round of applause at Mallory Square, the heat of the day still lingered and most people were either soaking in a pool or soaking up a cold one in a bar.

"Hi, one for dinner?" the girl at the door asked as he entered the restaurant.

"Yeah, got a table?" Jack joked lamely.

The place was empty.

"Follow me," she said, leading him to a nice spot on the patio. "This okay?"

"It's a little crowded," he joked again.

"Oh, I can seat you somewhere else," the girl said, taking him seriously. "Any place you like."

"I'm kidding. It's fine."

The girl blushed and smiled broadly.

"My name is Jennifer and I'll be your waitperson."

"Hello, Jennifer. I'm Jack and I'll be your customer. What's the special?"

"Baked sea bass with a crab stuffing and raspberry sauce severed on plantain," she recited.

"Sounds complicated. What would you suggest?"

"Personally, I'd go with a Caesar salad. And we got in a bunch of fresh shrimp this afternoon. Be great with it."

"Sold," Jack said. "And a glass of white wine."

"We have a nice Chablis, that okay?"

Jack said that it was fine, too, and when she had left, he

got up from the table for a look. It was clean. Mark up one in its favor. And the patio was certainly a romantic setting with green plantings placed around and perfect lighting. Number two in its favor. So where was everybody?

Jennifer returned with his glass of wine.

"It's so pretty out here," she said, taking in the patio herself as she placed the glass on the table. "I wish more people knew about it."

"Yes, it is," Jack agreed. "Why do you think they don't? Do you advertise?"

"We did at the beginning and were busy then but lately...I don't know," she shrugged.

"What changed?"

"People get fickle. At least, they do in Key West."

Jack nodded.

"I'll go check on your salad," she smiled brightly.

~~~

A balmy breeze had brought a little relief to the island and the sidewalks were fuller as Jack strolled along Duval. His salad at Stella by Starlight had been good. Jennifer was right about the fresh shrimp. And business had picked up— well, slightly— before he'd left. Three other tables. Billy was right, too. They needed to talk.

"Got any change you can spare, bro?" a shirtless man whispered from an alley.

Jack sighed and passed by without a word. He felt like crap for doing so but the guy would probably just use the money to buy a drink. Well, was that so wrong? He turned back to the alley. The man had disappeared.

Up ahead was Vinos. The narrow porch of the wine bar overlooked Duval Street and offered a choice location for people-watching. All the chairs were taken. Jack went inside to the bar.

The bar was full, too, but he was lucky and a guy got up to leave. He settled on the stool and caught the bartender's eye.

"What'll you have, honey?" she asked.

"Think I'll just do a beer."

Jack spotted Earl Gleason sitting at the end of the bar, seemingly lost in thought.

"Here's your beer, sweetie," the bartender said.

"I'll take it down to the end. See an old friend."

Jack made his way through the crowd.

"Been awhile, Earl," he greeted with a smile and a clap on the back. "How're you doing?"

Gleason snapped out of his reverie and groaned when he recognized who it was.

"My lucky night," he said. "In town for long, I hope not?"

The two men had an odd relationship. Their paths had first crossed when the detective was investigating a robbery at the Inedible Cafe. An immediate dislike flamed up between them and was later fanned by their mutual interest in the same woman. Ironically, they joined forces later to find the answer to some questionable deaths of children buried in the Key West cemetery.

"Just got in this morning," Jack grinned. "Took the redeye last night. But yeah, I might be here for awhile. LA's growing tiresome."

"I'm surprised," Gleason said. "I always figured you for the perennial Hollywood type."

"Disappointed you'd think that. I always considered you as being more perceptive."

Gleason laughed.

"Ah, I'm just breaking your balls, Jack."

"Anything or anyone new in your life?"

"Have a roommate now."

"No kidding? Guy? Girl?"

"Cat. Name's Mitts. Hemingway cat. Moved in awhile ago."

"Don't those cats have six toes?"

"You got it. So did his former owner."

"God, that's what I love about Key West."

~~~

Rachel Powers' washing machine was spewing water like a sick whale. She'd just put in a load of laundry and gone to the living room with a glass of wine when she heard a loud rumble followed by a big splash. Now water was all over the floor. She yanked the electric plug out of the socket to stop the stupid thing.

Last month it had been the hot water heater. The landlord had dickered around for a week before finally getting it replaced. No telling how long it'd be for this. Maybe she should just call a repair man. Get it fixed and save herself the grief. She took the soggy clothes out of the machine and dumped them in the kitchen sink.

She had rented the tiny house on Harris Avenue sight unseen. Well, there *was* a picture. It'd been advertised online by the owner and offered a price-break for military, both active and ex. That sounded good because anything else she might've considered in Key West was priced beyond imagination, much less affordability. She had some money saved but still needed to watch her pennies. Still, she'd had no idea of how expensive living in Key West could be.

Neither had her husband when he'd proposed the idea. He'd come to Key West on vacation years ago with his parents and fallen in love with the Lower Keys. It had always been his dream to retire down here after he'd put in his twenty. He was eight years short when his chopper went down during a night training mission in Arizona. Nine months later a suicide bomber almost made hash of her in Baghdad.

She decided to forego the glass of wine. Bed sounded more appealing. She was going to need all her wits about her the way this murder investigation seemed to be shaping up.

Chapter 6

A banner headline across the front page of *The Citizen* posed a question. "Serial Killer?" it blared.

"Oh, don't be so dramatic," the man said with a prissy smile before reading the story beneath it.

~~~

"Where'd they get this?" Jay Halderman asked. "I said to keep a lid on the serial killer business."

"Small island," Gleason shrugged. "You know how it goes. Someone slipped up or has a pal at the paper. Happens."

The two policemen were in the lieutenant's office.

"Yeah, yeah," Halderman said. "Thing is, we don't know if there's a serial killer. All we know is that we're investigating two homicides in the same area. Could be they're tied to the same individual but even that doesn't make him a serial killer. This sensational crap only causes panic. Where's Powers?"

"On her way. She had to stop by Sears to price washing machines. Hers blew up last night."

Halderman shook his head.

"How does a washing machine blow up?" he asked no one in particular.

~~~

Jack Hunter had a different response to the lead story as he sat on his front porch reading the newspaper. Memories welled up, both distant and recent.

He thought of the tough times he'd gone through as a homeless person in Key West. How unexpectedly it had happened to him. A business executive one day and a fugitive the next.

Homelessness. Living with constant fear. Harsh nights spent sleeping in the open. That moment the last of your money runs out. And the final blow, the realization that you've now vanished from one world and reappeared in another. No longer a productive individual, hardly considered a human being, just a burden at best.

Some homeless become predators and others prey. He remembered the poor homeless soul that had been murdered by the Satanic cult in Los Angeles. And how he'd resolved then to help those in need whenever possible.

~~~

Janice Irwin checked her makeup one more time in the rearview mirror. She'd heard that the guy who ran a concession stand at Smathers Beach might have a job opening. She was up for it, no matter what. It'd been five months since her last real paycheck. Three months since she'd lost her apartment. Well, ever since her boyfriend had kicked her out after he'd beat her up for the umpteenth time. Now she lived in her car, a battered old Pontiac that they didn't even make anymore. She just thanked God the thing still ran.

She'd wound up in Key West because it was as far as she could run away from the wreckage of a life built on abusive relationships which included two failed marriages.

She now eked out a living on an iffy income. Panhandling. Collecting bottles and aluminum cans for their deposits. On a really great day, she might score a few bucks putting up stock in one of the shops in the mall. Real work there.

That kept her in gas money. Very important to be mobile. Some of the shelters offered showers. She could get to a soup kitchen. And to the library where you could safely spend time, maybe exchange tips with others in the same fix as yourself and, praise be, use the bathroom unhindered. The laundromat was another good source for information on what was happening in her world.

She had to move the car every couple of days, too. Otherwise it'd be ticketed. Neighborhoods were the worst. People would call the cops as soon as they spotted you. Shopping centers offered the best parking but still you couldn't be too obvious. Again, keep on the move. She was good with the Sears lot for now.

She freshened her lipstick and offered a little prayer. A car pulled into the space next to her with a woman perhaps her age behind the wheel—as she herself might've once appeared before she moved to the street but certainly not now. They exchanged looks and the woman smiled back.

Maybe this would be her lucky day.

~~~

A Pacific storm had thrashed Los Angeles the night before but by morning had moved east, leaving the sky as clear as a perfect gin martini. The entire LA basin sparkled, but Benny Spring was enjoying none of the view from his office window. His day had been clouded by the appearance of an old client who'd shown up unannounced and unwanted while his secretary was out.

"I thought you were in prison," Benny said uncomfortably.

"It was all a mistake," Leonard Hall said. "So they let me out."

"Why would they do that?"

"Must've finally figured they had the wrong guy."

"Bullshit! I'm calling the cops," Benny snapped, reaching for his phone.

"Be my guest," Leonard said, patting his coat pocket. "I've got my release papers right here. All legit."

Benny looked at him warily. What else did he have in there, he wondered? The guy had changed since they'd last met. He'd been a scrawny punk then. He was bigger now. Meaner looking. There was a nasty vibe he was giving off, too.

"Nice office," Leonard said, taking in the room. "Smaller than your last one, though. Decline in business?"

"Got a nice deal," Benny said, shuffling some papers on his desk. "Lease was up on the old place. Century City had gotten stale, anyway. Action's back on the Strip now."

Leonard shook his head and smiled.

"You've gotten older, Benny," he said. "Don't remember you as being so grey."

Benny didn't reply. Leonard walked over to the window.

"Great view," he said, opening a sliding glass door and stepping out onto a small balcony. "Almost see the Hollywood sign from here."

"Yeah, well, Sunset Boulevard's like that," Benny said, his concern now growing. He stole a quick glance at his desk drawer where he kept a loaded gun.

"The girl who worked for you before?" Leonard asked, returning inside but leaving the door standing open. "She still here? What was her name?"

"Francine. She quit. Got a new girl now. In fact, she should be back any minute."

"I heard Francine became a cop. Actually, she was already one then. Did you know that about her? That she was a fucking cop? I didn't."

"She was just a part-time office squeeze," Benny said with a dismissive wave. "I didn't give a rat's ass about what she did on her own. She wanted to go play cop? Fine."

"Fine? Maybe it's fine with you but it wasn't so fine for me. I spent a thousand days in prison because your *squeeze* was a cop. Kind of makes me wonder if you set me up, huh? Like maybe the two of you were in on it. Yeah, she gets a promotion. And what did you get, Benny?"

Benny paled slightly. This guy was a nut case, he thought.

"Why would I have done that? I didn't know you were

wanted for murder at the time."

Leonard looked at him with dead eyes.

"Manslaughter, Benny, voluntary manslaughter not murder. Big difference between the two."

"Of course," Benny sneered. "But talk about wondering. I wonder if the husband of the woman you voluntarily slaughtered sees it that way. As that big difference you made so cleverly clear."

"I'll ask him that over dinner some night," Leonard smiled. "All right, let's get down to business. How much money do I have?"

Benny turned up his palms and grinned.

"Are we now playing a game? Am I supposed to guess?"

"Don't fuck with me, Benny. You know what I'm talking about. My script, remember?"

The Hollywood agent gave a little chuckle and got up from his desk and walked over to a side table where a pitcher of water stood.

"Care for a glass?" he asked, pouring himself one while he considered crashing the pitcher against Leonard's head.

"No, I just want what's owed me. That movie was going to be a blockbuster, right? Isn't that what you told me? A real blockbuster, you said. So? Where's the money?"

"Well, life is full of surprises," Benny said, setting down the water pitcher and feeling more in control. He could handle this.

"Eastern European production company bought the script. As far as what the movie grossed, who the hell knows? Goddamn commies kept everything. That's how they work."

"Then, let's talk about my script. Fuck the movie. They paid you for the script. How much?"

Benny laughed and shook his head.

"Nobody really wanted the damn thing, Leonard. Hate to tell you but it was the biggest joke in town. Nothing personal, mind you. This is a tough business. Gotta be a pro to survive in the industry. I was lucky to pawn off your lousy little script for as much as I did. Took the one and only offer as soon as they made it. For your information, I made zip after expenses."

"You expect me to believe that?" Leonard shouted. "That script was brilliant! Nothing like it had ever been written. Directors would've been falling all over themselves to get it."

"Dream on, my friend. By the way, there was no signed contract between us. If I remember, you had other more pressing obligations at the time."

Leonard glared menacingly at Benny.

"You owe me money. I don't like being cheated."

Benny applauded.

"Hey, that sounded great! I should get you an audition."

He was back on his game now. Who did this jerk think he was coming in here and trying to shake him down?

"Think I don't know how much you got paid?" Leonard raged. "Joke's on you, Benny. My lawyer reads the trades. I'm going to sue you."

"The line is, *I'll see you in court*," Benny laughed even harder. "Ever consider being a comedian? You're a natural."

Leonard grabbed Benny by the shoulders, pulling him out of his chair and slamming him hard against the wall. Benny was a slight man and it didn't take much.

"Let go of me!" Benny cried out. "I'll pay whatever you want!"

Leonard patted Benny on the cheek.

"See? I knew we could make a deal."

"I'll give you what money I have in the desk. I can write you a check for more."

Benny heaved a breath and went to his desk and pulled open the drawer. Only he didn't remove any cash. Instead, he grabbed out a .40 Sig Sauer pistol.

Leonard was on top of him before he could even take aim. He painfully bent back Benny's wrist, breaking it, and then pushed him out onto the balcony.

"I'll consider this payment in full," he hissed, throwing him over the rail.

Benny barely had time to scream before hitting the pavement at eighty-five miles per hour.

Leonard quickly stepped back inside, picked up the gun off the floor and slipped it into his pocket. He looked in the open desk drawer and found an envelope full of cash. He stuck it in another pocket. Benny's suit jacket hung on the back of the door. He rummaged through it, discovered his billfold and put it in his hip pocket. As an afterthought, he pulled out a tissue from a box on a side table and wiped off the front of the desk drawer. He then looked around the office to see if there were any other places he might've left fingerprints. Satisfied that there were none, he left the office unseen and took the stairway steps to the ground floor, where he calmly exited the building as an LAPD patrol car crawled through the stopped traffic on Sunset Boulevard toward a gathering horrified crowd.

He threw back his head and swiftly walked away. He felt great.

Chapter 7

"Thinking about getting myself a motor scooter, Billy."

"A dose of road rash is what you'll get, hee-hee. Scooter's dangerous. People falling off 'em every day down here."

Jack and Billy were at the Inedible Cafe. They'd finished serving breakfast and Billy was mopping the kitchen floor.

"Finding it hard to peddle that ol' bicycle around these days?" he grinned. "Old man age's catching up, huh."

Jack shrugged.

"Just something with a motor would be more efficient," he said. "Get where you're going quicker."

"Hell, Jack, this island's only four miles long by two miles wide, hee-hee. How soon do you want to get where you're going anyway?"

"Something I'm thinking about, is all," Jack replied petulantly.

"Since we're talking about efficiency," Billy said, "think I'm wasting my time having to mop this damn floor. Should be getting ready for lunch or doing something about Stella by Starlight."

"I ate there last night," Jack said. "Passed on the special. Went for a salad instead at Jennifer's recommendation. She seems pretty sharp, by the way."

"She's a smart girl. But right now what we need is a chef."

"Well, that's your department, Billy. Tell you what, though, I've got an idea for getting you some more help around here."

"Don't need any wait-folks, Jack. Need a bottle washer and a mop jockey. People don't want low-paying jobs anymore."

"Untapped workforce right out there on the street, Billy."

~~~

"Get your washer squared away?" Gleason asked.

He and Powers were seated at their desks in the detective's room. The morning briefing with Halderman was over by the time she'd finally gotten in.

"Think it might be cheaper to buy a new one," Powers said. "Sir, I'm sorry about being late this morning. It won't happen again."

Gleason laughed.

"Hey, no big deal. Lieutenant's cool. Sears got the best price? I don't even know what a washer costs. I take all of my things to the laundromat."

"I probably should take mine, too," she smiled, "but the machine came with the house and the landlord is so slow to do anything. Easier just to handle it myself."

She winced as a jolt of pain suddenly shot up her spine. It happened more frequently now that she'd decided to ween herself off the medication.

Gleason had caught the expression.

"You all right?" he asked.

"I must've pulled a muscle cleaning up all that water last night."

"If you buy that washer and need someone to hook it up, let me know. Save you a couple of bucks."

"Thank you, sir."

Gleason took in a breath.

"You're welcome," he smiled. "Now, here's some good news. We have a name for our last victim at the Blue Bayou. Scott Endress. Got a hit from NCIC this morning. He was arrested for burglary in Louisiana. Some place called Raquelle Harbor. Here's his picture."

"That's outstanding, sir."

"Check back with the shelter. Maybe they know him."

~~~

It hadn't been a pleasant ride to the homeless shelter. Traffic was heavy on both the street and the bike lane. Thermometer read 84 degrees, felt like 148.

"You'll need to sign in," the woman at the intake desk told him when he entered.

"I'm not staying. But I'd like some information."

"Sure, what can I help you with? If there are other community services you need, I can give you a list."

Jack wondered if he looked that bad. He realized that the ride had taken a lot out of him, but still.

"My name's Jack Hunter. I live in town and might have a job for one or two of your people."

"By our people you must mean our clients," she corrected good-naturedly.

"I hadn't really thought of it that way. I didn't mean to offend."

"I'm Dorothy Rowe," she said. "What kind of job are you talking about? Maybe I'd be interested."

"Mopping the floor, sweeping up, maybe some kitchen duties," Jack said. "My business partner runs a couple of restaurants and could use some help."

"Why come here?" Dorothy asked. "He should put an ad in the paper."

Jack explained what had brought him there and what he had in mind.

"That's a wonderful thing," Dorothy said, "but it might be a large order. Most of the homeless come here from out of the county. Many of them have gotten used to their situation and have given up on trying to do anything about it. A lot have mental problems, too. We offer a safe place to sleep. That's about it. I think you might be better off checking with some of the assisted living places and transitional housing."

That was something Jack hadn't considered. When he was homeless in Key West, he couldn't have chanced staying anywhere that might've offered help. He'd been on the run from the law then. Shelter like this had to be on the regular beat for cops. His thought was interrupted by another person entering the office.

"Detective Powers," Dorothy said brightly. "Good to see you again."

Jack turned to see a woman with dark hair bracketing a sweet face. She had on a tailored charcoal pants suit that showed off a trim body. There was something else about her that he couldn't quite put his finger on.

"Nice of you to remember me, Dorothy," Powers said. "Just when you have a moment, no hurry."

She had an engaging smile, Jack thought to himself. And she's a detective? Probably knows Gleason.

"Good day, sir," she said to Jack. "I didn't mean to break in on your business. Please continue."

"I had about finished," he said. "You go ahead."

She flashed him a smile and turned her attention back to Dorothy.

"Do you recognize this person?" she asked, holding up a photograph. "His name is Scott Endress, if that helps."

Dorothy studied the picture.

"No, is he the one you...uh...found?"

"Yes."

Dorothy pursed her lips and gave a sad little nod.

"I'll see if he has ever registered here. Like I said, you have to sign in even if it's only for one night. By the way, that other man you were asking about? Richard Kirby? Well, I checked with the manager and he said that Mr. Kirby had been asked to leave."

"Drugs or fighting?"

"He didn't say. I don't see any record of a Scott Endress. He might've just lived on the street. Or maybe someone took him in."

"Maybe the street but I doubt the other," Powers said. "Still, anything's possible, I guess."

"I once knew a homeless guy who did exactly that," Jack said.

Powers looked at him and cocked her head slightly.

"He lived on the street until someone took him in."

"Really?" she said, the smile not so engaging this time. "Are you connected with the shelters?"

"No, I'm here to find some help."

"And this is where you come for that?"

A lop-sided grin suddenly creased Jack's face. It was an old habit that never did him any good.

"It's a long story, Detective Powers," he said. "You wouldn't be interested."

"Oh, I wouldn't say that, sir," She said "But how do you know my name and that I am a detective? Have we met before?"

Jack now wished to Heaven he'd left the minute this woman had walked in.

"I heard Dorothy call you that when you came in. I'm Jack Hunter. Do you know Earl Gleason? He's a friend."

"Yes, I do and I'll be sure to mention you to him."

Jack thanked her and left.

Chapter 8

"**H**omicide, this is Detective Dalton."

"Detective Dalton, it's Francine Mason. Remember me?"

Dalton was at her desk in the detective's room at Van Nuys Division. It had been a long day and the department was short-handed. Detective Jason Rivers was still on medical leave. Last thing she needed now was a social chat.

"Hi, Francine, what's up?"

She'd met Mason when the two of them were working West LA. Dalton had been a Detective One then and Mason was a reserve officer on the desk. She had helped Dalton and her partner in a homicide case and later went back to the Police Academy and became a regular. She now worked patrol at Hollywood.

"Did you hear about that jumper on Sunset?" she asked.

"Not really. We've been up to our fannies. I've got three gangbangers and an ADW just came in. Guy beat up his partner with a rolling pin, if you can imagine. They were taking a cooking class together. My D-One's gone for another month, so I'm all by my lonesome. The boss is going apeshit."

Detectives are divided into three ranks in the LAPD. Detective one is the designation given to a patrol officer moving up to the squad. Dalton's D-One was Jason Rivers, who'd been seriously injured in a motorcycle accident. Detective Three Tom Bradshaw was head of homicide at Van Nuys. Dalton, herself, was a Detective Two, a rank that put her more in the trenches than running the shop. She hoped to keep it that way.

"So what's with the jumper?"

"This is actually kind of upsetting for me," Francine said, lowering her voice a notch. "Do you remember Benny Spring? I worked for him when I was a reserve at West LA."

"Of course I do. And I still appreciate your help with the Ridenour case. Why do you ask?"

"He jumped out of his office window this morning."

"Oh, Francine. Certainly, this must be upsetting. But isn't he in Century City? I mean, how'd he do it? You can't open those windows."

"He'd apparently moved to the Strip some time ago. His new office had a little balcony. Right now it's an unclassified death. The detectives are investigating. Probably determine it was a suicide. Yeah, Benny was Mister Hollywood but that's just the business, you know? I remember how he used to visit that old actor friend who lived at the retirement home. That was a side of him he kept private. Are you still seeing your friend? The guy who was involved in that case?"

"You're obviously talking about Jack Hunter," Dalton said. "And no, I never was *seeing* him, as you put it."

"Oh, I didn't mean anything," Francine apologized.

Dalton waited a beat before continuing.

"Forget it," she laughed. "What the hell, yeah, we went out a couple of times but it wasn't like we were an item or something. Anyway, he's not in town. Things move on."

"Okay, I won't keep you. Still, I can't get over Benny. Never thought he'd do something like that. Guess you never know, huh? Take care."

After she'd hung up, Dalton considered what Mason had said about Benny Spring. She remembered that story about his visiting a friend at the old actor's home. Imagine, a Hollywood agent with a heart! Then he takes a nose dive out of a window. Too true, you never know what's really going on with people.

And now Jack Hunter was brought up. What had she just told Francine? Things move on. She shook her head and went back to work on the rolling pin caper.

~~~

"I'm giving Endress's photo to patrol," Gleason said. "They can show it around. Someone might remember seeing him."

He and Powers were at the station discussing the day's progress in the two homicides. They hadn't much to show for all of their running around.

"Sorry I struck out with the shelters, sir," Powers said. "No one recognized him at any of the places I went."

"Nothing to be sorry about, Rachael, doesn't mean he was never there. Just they don't remember him, that's all."

She smiled.

"Guess they do tend to blend together. Seen one...you know the rest. Still, it *is* a small homeless community here. You'd think someone would know. Especially with Kirby since he'd been around for awhile. Maybe it's just distrust of cops."

Gleason took in a breath and let it out.

"Thing is, I'd like to connect the two homicides. Could be a piece of a bigger puzzle. I feel in my gut there's something going on between them. Not necessarily to do with drugs, either."

"What about the wound pattern comparison you were thinking about?" she asked.

"Nothing back from the medical examiner yet on Endress," Gleason said. "He probably thinks I'm nuts for even suggesting a connection."

"Well, I think it could be important, sir," Powers said. "I've read a little about the comparison of patterns. Generally males are involved with knives and clubs. Our homicides seem to fit the victim ages in both causes of death. But it kind of goes astray with locations. Knife seem to be the weapon of choice outdoors and clubs are preferred for indoors. Weird, huh?"

37

Gleason shrugged.

"There were no defensive wounds on Kirby," he said. "I thought that unusual. No cuts on the hands or arms."

"Maybe he was first attacked from behind," Powers suggested. "Murderer stabbed him in the back. Could've been fatal or at least disabling. Subsequent wounds were done purely out of rage. Not unlike what happened with Endress."

"Possibly," Gleason nodded. "Thing about him dealing could have something to do with it but I don't know. Crime just doesn't seem to fit a drug deal."

"You want another cup of coffee, sir?" Powers asked. "I'm going to the machine."

"No, I'm about to float away on what I've already drunk. Thanks."

Gleason, lost in thought, drummed his fingers on the desk top. Powers could be right, he admitted to himself. Or maybe all of this wound pattern stuff was just hocus-pocus bullshit. Suppose both killings were the results of fights that'd gone over the top? Very likely hypothesis.

"Met a friend of yours today," Powers said, returning. "Jack Hunter."

This snapped Gleason out of his daydreaming.

"Where was that?"

"At the KOTS. He was looking for help."

Gleason shook his head in amazement.

"Why am I not surprised? Did he say what kind of help he hoped to find?"

"I asked Dorothy Rowe about it after he'd left. She works the intake desk. Told me he was there looking to hire someone for his buddy's restaurant. Sound okay to you? Seems kind of strange to me."

"No, that sounds like Hunter. It's true about the restaurant. He and his pal own a couple of them in town. That's how we first ran into each other. I was investigating a robbery a couple of years ago that had taken place in one of them. Named the Inedible Cafe, if you can believe that. We've crossed paths many times since."

Powers took that in.

"Did they catch the bad guy in the robbery?" she asked.

"Yeah, he denied it at first. Tried to say the victim made a pass at him and even pulled a gun. The vic was Hunter's bud. Turned out to be a nice enough guy. Hunter got all bent out of shape. Thought I came down too hard on his pal."

"I was interested in why he was at the shelter since he wasn't one of their guests," Powers said. "Wondered if it might have anything to do with our case. What's he like, this friend of yours?"

Gleason rolled his eyes.

"Trouble. He has a knack for it."

"I see."

"Don't get me wrong, he's a good guy. He even saved my butt once. But like the Boy Scouts say, be prepared whenever Jack Hunter's involved."

Powers sipped her coffee and let that one sink in.

~~~

Jack had come home after visiting the shelter on Stock Island. It'd been a long, hot bike ride and he'd walked straight into the shower. Now, a little more refreshed, he was taking an easy stroll over to the Bight.

He headed down Southard Street and hung a right on Grinnell, passing some of the beautifully restored houses. It was always a great walk. But his mind was elsewhere. He'd become aware of something missing since he'd returned. The old characters. Those off-kilter people, the eclectic and eccentrics—sweet souls who'd been such an important part of his life before. And, in his opinion, had added to the charm of Key West. Where had they gone?

Some had left town, of course. Bobby Sunshine, Ruth LaVere, Ruby Steele. Astrid Kelly? Well, she could turn up any time, not that he'd be all that happy to see her. Still. Memories stepping out from the shadows.

The sun dropped behind the cruise ships docked at Mallory Square. He continued along the boardwalk, the bars still crowded from afternoon. He came to where he could look across the water to the Galleon. A small group had gathered at the little Tiki, bursts of laughter shot from it. But rather than join the conviviality, he decided to continue up Front Street.

Now he faced more options. Happy hour was underway at the Chart Room. The whole of Lower Duval awaited him. He hailed a passing taxi.

"I'm going to the Inedible Cafe," he told the driver. "You know where it is?"

The man nodded that he did.

Jack sat back in the seat as the cab pulled away. This was calamari night and Billy might need some help.

~~~

There'd been no job at the concession stand. But that hadn't kept the man who ran it from propositioning her. She should've reported him to the cop on the beat, she'd berated herself. But what good would that have done? The jerk would've denied it and she would've been made to look like a fool.

No, she thought that she had done the right thing by going back to her car and driving away before she got a parking ticket. It wasn't as if it'd been the first time she'd been hit on like that. Men are quick to size up a homeless woman as being easy. Amazingly, they felt they were doing you a favor.

She was heading to the soup kitchen when the Pontiac's engine began to stumble. She checked the fuel gauge. Running on fumes. She pulled into a gas station and put in eight bucks worth of regular. That would have to do.

She had planned to stick around the kitchen until lunch.

Then she'd volunteer to help clean up afterwards. Volunteers got divvies on any leftovers.

However, she'd ended up spending the entire day there. And it had turned out to be her lucky day, after all. Several rooms were being renovated and one of the painters had called in sick. She offered to fill in for him, fibbing some about her experience. But they had been satisfied with her work and had actually paid her!

Now she was parked in her old spot at the shopping center with a little extra money in her purse. The lot was nearly full and the stores were doing a good business. She decided to window shop before bedding down for the night.

She was just walking past Sears when a man overtook her from behind.

"Excuse me, miss," he said.

Her heart fell. Was this going to be another sleazy proposition?

He was a middle-aged man dressed in nice slacks and a collared golf shirt and wore sunglasses. He looked vaguely familiar. He might've worked in one of the stores.

"I just bought this sandwich from the restaurant and my wife called to say we were going out for dinner," he said, holding up a paper bag. "I don't mean to be presumptuous, but would you like to have it? It's chicken salad and they made it fresh."

She smiled. People often offered food to those less fortunate. She was grateful for their kindness. Looks like her lucky day wasn't over yet.

"Why, thank you," she said. "That's awfully nice."

"My pleasure," he said.

She went back to her car and got into the rear seat where she slept. That sandwich should hit the spot, she thought, unwrapping it and taking a big bite.

Within seconds, Janice Irwin was dead.

Chapter 9

He'd turned to the internet for information about serial murders. Who looks for this stuff? He certainly never had. Sure, you hear about serial killers but it wasn't a subject fascinating enough to require further study. Unless you were involved.

He needed to find out what he was up against, get as much info on the subject as the cops had.

His first question was what's the difference between a serial killer and, say, some nutcase walking into a school and shooting everybody?

Simply put, serial murder was the unlawful killing of two or more victims by the same offender in separate events. The other would be classified as mass murder.

The answer, oddly enough, made him feel uncomfortable. He'd certainly never thought of it that way. Wouldn't even have been looking up the subject had it not been for that sensational story in the newspaper.

He read further and discovered that there was no single identifiable cause that led to the development of a serial killer. Well, he begged to differ. It'd been the elephant in his room most of his damn life.

So what did they think *was* behind a person becoming one, he wondered. Clicking to another site he found the answer. Serial killers are driven by their own unique motives or reasons. Oh, yes! It explained that there were multiple factors involved and the most significant was the serial killer's personal decision to go ahead with the crime.

Yet the whole idea of him being a serial killer was kind of hard to swallow. He had to admit some of the profile characteristics sort of fitted him. Especially the part about lack of remorse. He wasn't one bit sorry. Most of the rest was bullshit, as far as he was concerned. Even contradicted itself half the time.

For instance, the experts contended that these people aren't monsters or misfits. To the contrary, they often have families, homes and jobs. In other words, just your plain average Joe Blow. They aren't deranged, either.

Yet, these same learned shrinks turn right around and get into all this psychopathy stuff. Predatory behavior. Need for control. Failure to accept responsibility. That last one was particularly galling. Responsibility? That'd been his middle name for fucking ever!

No, he had a very definite reason for playing his little game and it had nothing to do with sexual repression, thrill seeking, or social deviance either. This was evening up the score. Giving some payback for a shitload of heartache. So fuck those know-it-alls.

They did have a point about the timing, though. Generally, they mentioned there being a break-in time between murders. A cooling-off period for the emotions to reset.

After he'd shot the first worthless drug-dealing punk at the beach, he had backed off for a while. Let things settle down before going on with his plan. Hey, who wouldn't have been a little upset? He'd never killed anyone before.

It had been during this very cooling-off period that a better idea had hit him. And a much more interesting one. Be creative with how you take out these pieces of shit. Different strokes for different folks. Keep the cops guessing. Make them chase their tails. Put some method in it. He had everything worked out, down to the last victim. Then he'd quit. Never do another.

So...laissez le bon temps roulez!

Chapter 10

"Thanks for the help last night, Jack. Must've cooked half an ocean full of calamari, hee-hee."

Jack had returned to the Inedible Cafe this morning after spending a long evening there waiting tables and washing dishes. Breakfast was about over and he and Billy were standing in the back alley.

"Well, at least the fire department didn't show up," Jack laughed.

Once before on a calamari night, a puff of smoke had billowed from the kitchen into the dining room, causing a near panic and a visit by engine number one.

"Yes sir-ee," Billy continued. "I would've been in a whole heap of trouble if you hadn't come by. Shorthanded here. Gonna get worse, too, if we don't start doing something soon."

"I was at the homeless shelter yesterday," Jack said.

"Lady took back her house, huh?" Billy winked. "You should've told me you need a place to stay."

"No, no, it's nothing like that," Jack laughed. "Thing I was mentioning the other day about that available workforce. Remember?"

"You talking homeless folks?"

"Yes, we could place a couple in both restaurants. Train them. You know, waitperson, kitchen help, that sort of work. Be a good thing to do, too."

Billy shook his head in amazement.

"You can't be serious, Jack. Nothing but addicts and burnouts at the shelter. Rejects. People just passing through on their way to nowhere."

"Well, that's just the point, Billy," he said testily.

"Maybe we can help them get somewhere."

"Now you're talking riddles, Jack. Let's go inside and have a cup of coffee."

The restaurant had completely cleared out and Billy got a couple cups of coffee and brought them to an empty table.

"You know, I was homeless when I came to Key West," Jack said, pulling back a chair and sitting. "Cecil gave me a break when he hired me to work here. Remember that time?"

"Sure I do," Billy smiled. "And with my training, you turned out to be a pretty good dishwasher."

"Scalded me in hot water, that's all you did," Jack said. "But seriously, now I want to return the favor. Give someone else a chance."

Billy took his time considering that before speaking.

"You're a fine person," he said. "I could see that in you the first time we met. But I don't think what you're saying now is a good idea. Times've changed since back then. Different kind of folks on the streets now. Gotten mean as all hell. Got to be careful about taking in strays."

"Not all of them are bad," Jack countered. "People often wind up homeless because of reasons they couldn't control. Jobs disappeared or are outsourced. Rich get richer, poor get poorer, that's the big divide. Yeah, some of them you can't help. They're too fargone. I'm interested in helping those you can."

"Why don't you just make a donation to the shelter, Jack? Do more good than hiring some drug addict to come in here."

"Not that many homeless are addicts, Billy. Don't have money to buy drugs."

"So you want to give them that money, huh?"

"No, I want them to earn it through a good-paying job. Put some respect back in their lives."

"Jack, I know you mean well about doing good for those

folks but the homeless people are big a problem here in Key West. Not everybody's up for taking them in. Most are ready to see them leave town. You want to understand why, just go down Duval Street any morning around daybreak. Be careful where you step otherwise you might fall over one."

"It's not something that's going away, Billy. You can't just close your eyes to the problem."

"Pay attention, Jack. There's a serial killer on the loose out there, knocking off homeless folks. More likely one of their own behind it. And you're talking about bringing 'em in here?"

A couple pushed through the door. Tourists.

"Still serving breakfast?" the man asked.

"Yes, sir," Billy said, jumping up from the table. "You all sit any place you like."

The woman walked over to a glass display case filled with plastic replicas.

"What are all of these?" she asked curiously.

"That's the menu," Billy told her. "Why they call this place the Inedible Cafe. Just point to what you want. Same thing with the Undrinkable Bar, hee-hee."

She gave him an odd look.

"We have printed menus, too," Jack said, placing a couple on their table. "Like some coffee?"

~~~

"Patrol picked up a shoplifter at the Mall last night," Halderman read from a report. "Perp trying to steal a bottle of twelve-year old scotch from the liquor store. Manager caught him stuffing it in a backpack."

He had Gleason and Powers in his office.

"Twelve-year old scotch." Gleason said gravely. "Capital offense."

Halderman cut his eyes at him. Powers hid a smile.

"Homeless guy by the name of Tyler Bain," he continued. "Tried it before at the same store according to the manager."

"Manager pressing charges?" Gleason asked.

"It's up in the air right now. Guy doesn't want the hassle but thinks maybe a night in jail would teach him a lesson."

"Ah, another hopeless naiveté. So what are *we* doing in here, boss?"

Halderman put down the report.

"Our shoplifter, fearing that the CA might get tough this time, told the officers he has some information about the Endress homicide."

~~~

Billy hadn't been all that impressed by Jack's idea of hiring the homeless to work at the restaurants. And now Jack was having second thoughts himself as he peddled down Truman.

He stopped for the red light at Simonton. Run it only if you have a death wish. Across the intersection a young girl on a motor scooter pulled out of the Moped Hospital and buzzed away, loose blonde hair flowing behind her.

The Moped Hospital was a former gas station that now rented, sold and repaired bicycles and motor scooters. Not where they take you if you have an accident on one. Rows of new scooters lined the lot facing Truman. A brightly painted red one called to Jack. The light turned green and he went straight for the lot.

"That beauty just came in," an affable man commented, walking up. "Put it out this morning. I'm Henry."

Jack stood up from where he'd been squatting for a closer look at the machine.

"Nice scooter," he said admiringly.

"Has that vintage look but without the headaches," Henry pointed out. "You live in town?"

"Yeah, I do."

"It's perfect for down here," Henry said. "Gets about eighty-five miles to the gallon on regular gas."

"You have any literature?"

"Sure. Hang on a moment while I go to the office. Why don't you sit on the scooter and see how it feels?"

Jack seated himself and wrapped his fingers around the hand grips. It was a perfect fit. He squeezed the brake levers and bounced the suspension. Firm. The instrument panel held a speedometer, clock and fuel gauge. But the neatest trick was the luggage box behind the seat. He began to smile. He felt like a kid.

"Here you go," Henry said, handing Jack a brochure.

"Thanks. How long would it take to get this thing ready?"

"Well, we can set up the financing and do the licensing. You can be riding this afternoon."

"Let me think about it."

"Don't wait too long. They go fast, and I'm not talking about its speed."

Jack said he'd call one way or the other.

Chapter 11

"**W**e can't hold this guy for more than twenty-four hours," Halderman reminded the two detectives, "unless the store manager decides to press charges."

He stood outside an interview room at the police station with Gleason and Powers. Tyler Bain waited inside.

"I know," Gleason said. "Let's go see what he has to say."

Gleason and Powers entered the room. Bain sat in a chair behind a table facing the door with his head down and arms folded around him. He looked up.

"Mr. Bain, I'm Detective Earl Gleason and this is Detective Rachael Powers. We appreciate your willingness to talk with us."

They took a seat across from him.

Gleason sized up the man. Average build. Probably early twenties. Had that raw, weathered look of chronic homelessness, which was odd for a person his age. Shifty, too.

"How are you today, sir?" Gleason asked. "Treating you all right?"

"Been better. Didn't get any damn sleep. People yelling all night."

"Well, I admit this isn't the best hotel in town," Gleason smiled. "Where are you from, Mr. Bain?"

"Hattiesburg, Mississippi" he said proudly. "Born and raised."

"Still have people there?"

"Uncles and aunts, cousins by the dozens, heh."

"Good to have family," Gleason said. "Now, let's get down to the reason we're all here. And again, we thank you for agreeing to see us. Mr. Bain, we're investigating the

51

murder of Scott Endress. And we understand you have some information for us, is that true?"

Bain swallowed.

"What's in it for me if I tell?" he asked slyly.

"Detective Powers?" Gleason smiled, gesturing toward her. "Answer that question for Mr. Bain, please."

"Tyler, we can talk with the City Attorney about your present situation," Powers said smoothly, "but if you are involved in the murder, we can't promise you anything."

Bain jumped to his feet, eyes wide.

"What the fuck are you talking about, lady? I didn't fucking kill nobody!"

Powers paused for a moment to let things settle down. She didn't want to scare him to death. He could clam up at any time. They couldn't afford that.

"I was only being honest with you, Tyler," she said calmly. "I have to say what I just told you. Department regulations. No one's accusing you of anything, okay? You do want us to be straight with you, don't you?"

"Just don't blame me for him being dead, that's all!"

Bain sat back down, a defiant expression still on his face.

"Why don't you start at the beginning, Tyler," Powers suggested. "That's always the best place. Tell us about Scott."

"We had a camp at the Blue Bayou."

"Just you and Scott?"

"We were all three there."

Gleason leaned forward. Here was a new twist.

"All three of you were there," Powers repeated. "Who was the third person?"

"Dick Kirby. He got kicked out the same time as me. So we made the camp together."

Halderman had been watching the video feed from the room. "Jesus Christ," he muttered. "Kirby was the first poor bastard killed in that goddamned place. And they were campmates?"

"Richard Kirby was also murdered out there," Powers said cautiously. "Do you know anything about that?"

"Somebody stuck him's what I heard. I was in jail when it happened. Got thirty days for nothing."

This was becoming incredible, Powers thought to herself.

"All right, going back to the homeless shelter," she said. "Why did you and Kirby have to leave?"

"Kirby sold pills. Then some stupid shit told one of the staff. Kirby found out who it was and beat the fuck out of him and that was all she wrote for us."

"Okay, now you and Kirby have set up camp at the Bayou, when did Scott Endress join you?"

"After I got out of jail. We'd seen each other around. I'd run into him on the street. Since Kirby was gone, I asked if he wanted to come stay with me. Told him it was a hell of a lot of fun out there. Plenty of partying and nobody to fuck with you."

New roomie moved into the very place where his buddy had been murdered, Powers thought to herself. How callous was that?

"Help me out here, Tyler," she said. "You and Endress were now living at the same campsite when Kirby was alive, is that right?"

"Oh, hell no. We made another camp. I wouldn't want to stay *there*."

Powers smiled. There was some hope for humanity.

"Tyler, when you said 'nobody to fuck with you' at the Bayou, exactly what did you mean?"

"You're on your own there. No rules or snitches. You know, do your own thing."

"Does that include being free to sell drugs?" Powers said. "No one to snitch on you? That what you and Endress were up to?"

She realized she was coming on too hard. She only hoped that Bain wouldn't freak out again. Instead, he snorted a little laugh.

"I learnt my lesson the first time, lady" he said, a sudden touch of fear in his voice. "Jail's no place for me. I wouldn't wish that on my worst enemy. No, ma'am, no way was I going to be dealing drugs and get sent back to jail."

Powers wondered about the reason for his dread of incarceration. Was it more than just being locked up?

"But you and Kirby dealt them when you were both at the Bayou, right?"

"Yeah, but then I was the one that got caught, wasn't I?"

Powers paused for a moment.

"How about Scott when he came to live there?" she asked. "Did he start dealing?"

"He did some. Hadn't learnt his lesson yet."

She paused again, looking at him sadly.

"I think he got more of a lesson than he deserved," Powers said quietly. "Don't you?"

Bain didn't reply.

"You are being very helpful, Tyler," she told him. "Let's keep going, okay?"

Bain smiled.

"We've talked about Richard Kirby and we know what happened to him," she said. "And we know how you and Scott came to be living at the Blue Bayou. Now is the time to tell us what you know about Scott's murder."

Halderman focused all of his attention on the television monitor outside. Bain sat wordlessly.

"You found Scott and told the cab driver, didn't you?" Powers said softly. "I bet the driver could identify you."

Bain got a wild look in his eyes and started to get up from the table.

"It's alright, Tyler, you're in no trouble. It was good that you reported it. You didn't have to wait for the police to arrive."

"His head was smashed in," Bain mumbled shakily.

"I can imagine how upsetting finding your friend like that must've been," she said. "Who do you think did that terrible thing to Scott? Anyone at the Blue Bayou?"

Bain heaved a breath.

"Could've been the guy wanting to buy."

She glanced quickly at Gleason, who was sitting quietly with his hands clasped in his lap. He nodded for her to continue.

"Did you recognize this man?" she asked.

"Hadn't seen him before. Scott and me was standing by the bridge. Couple boys camped across the Bayou was planning on a party and we thought maybe we'd go. Guy came up and asked if we could help him out, you know? Scott asked what he was wanting. Man said he was looking to buy some pills. Scott took him back to our camp. I figured he might be going to rob the fellow, he did that sometimes. So I went on to the party."

"Pills, huh?" Gleason commented. "Drugs in the Keys are now pharmaceuticals."

"Was this man who wanted to buy the drugs also homeless?" Powers continued. "Did he live at the Bayou?"

"Like I said, never seen him before. He was just kind of regular looking. White guy. Little bigger than me. But he wasn't homeless. I mean, he was dressed like he might've been. Worn-out clothes and all, but I could tell he wasn't really."

Powers felt a chill creep up body.

"How did you know that, Tyler?"

"He had a good haircut."

~~~

The detectives had gathered in Halderman's office to discuss their interview with Bain.

"You still think that serial killer idea is bullshit?" Gleason asked. "We've got two dead bodies found at the same general scene."

"It doesn't fit the profile," Halderman contended. "Too many outliers. All we've got right now are coincidences. Two homeless victims. You agree, Rachel?"

"Could be three victims, sir," she said. "Didn't that shooting near the beach also involve a homeless person?"

"Yeah, but that was obviously a soured drug deal," Halderman said. "Big gap between then and now. Different location. Plus, like you said, it was a shooter there. These latest two are entirely separate. One stabbing. The other blunt force. Serial killer usually uses the same method."

Powers considered his argument.

"Hmmm...I read the coroner's report on the gunshot victim," she said. "Just curious, you know. The man at the beach was riddled with wounds. Bit of overkill there, wouldn't you say? Now we have two more murdered in a frenzy. Overkill. I think there *might be* a tie between them."

Gleason was impressed by the idea a connection. Especially the overkill similarity.

"That's good work, detective," he said.

"Thank you, sir."

"We should've spotted that," Gleason said to Halderman. "The shooting vic had ten slugs in him. Apparently from a revolver since there weren't any casings. Fucking pyscho had to reload."

"So you're saying one person might be responsible for all three homicides?" he asked Powers.

"It had occurred to me," she said. "The extreme manner in which they were each committed is what stands out—the brutality—even though different weapons were used, which I admit is odd. Still it was as if the murderer wanted to obliterate his victim."

Halderman studied her.

"This mysterious drug buyer posing as a homeless," he said, "you think he may be Scott Endress's killer? Other than Tyler Bain, he *was* the last person to see him alive, as far as we know."

"If so—and I think it's a strong possibility that he is— then this could *well* be a serial killer," Powers said. "It's the most sinister thing I've ever been involved with."

Gleason grunted.

"What do we do about Tyler Bain?" he asked. "The liquor store manager isn't going to press charges. I think we've gotten about everything we're going to. Wouldn't count on him identifying the homeless actor. Cut him loose?"

"City Attorney won't take the case without a charge," Halderman said. "Sure, let him go."

"Here's another idea," Gleason said. "All things considered, he does qualify for the one-way program."

"What's that, sir?" Powers asked curiously.

"You get a one-way bus ticket to anywhere in the country with the proviso that you don't come back here," Halderman explained. "Otherwise, we'll pick you up."

"Might be good karma to reunite Tyler with his folks in Mississippi," Gleason grinned. "For sure it gets him out of our hair."

Chapter 12

Jack brought his bicycle into the house. It was safer inside than leaving it on the porch. Even in nice neighborhoods and with locks on their wheels, bikes were known to disappear without notice.

He opened the refrigerator, pulled out a beer and took it to the backyard which now offered a little shade. Relaxing in a lawn chair, he read the brochure Henry had given him.

No question about that red number—it was the one for him. He checked out the specifications. Hell, he didn't know why he was sitting around! He took out his cell phone.

"Moped Hospital. Jimmy speaking."

"This is Jack Hunter. Henry there?"

"No, he had to go home."

"Okay, I was talking with him earlier about that red Kymco scooter on your lot. Think I might be interested."

"Someone's looking at it right now."

"Tell them it's already sold. I'll be there as soon as I can with a check. Leaving the house as we speak."

Jack ended the call and ran back inside to get his bike. He figured the quickest route would be Angela and past the cemetery to Truman, then a line drive to Simonton. He made it in twenty minutes. His breath caught up with him a few seconds later.

The red motor scooter sat in the same place where he'd last seen it. His heart beat faster. He walked into the office.

"Hi, can I help you?" a young man asked.

"Yes, are you Jimmy? I'm Jack Hunter. Just spoke with you about that red scooter out there."

"It's all yours if you what it," Jimmy replied cheerfully. "The other fella walked away."

Jack grinned happily. Billy wouldn't like it but Billy would just have to worry.

~~~

Tyler Bain resisted the offer at first but Lieutenant Jay Halderman convinced him that it was one he couldn't afford not to take. He was due to leave town in the next few days on a bus for Miami and points west. If in future, they needed him for an ID, they could always bring him back or shoot a photo line-up to the PD in his hometown. Gleason and Powers were sitting at their desks in the detective's room.

"I wish we had a better description of that guy," she said wistfully. "Worn-out clothes and a good haircut aren't much to go on."

"Dress him in some new clothes," Gleason shrugged. "See if that helps. Actually, I'm not kidding. The old ones may have just been a disguise. Bain said he was average, little bigger than himself, and had a great coif. So we start there. Only with a better wardrobe."

She smiled at the mentioning of a coif.

"I was also thinking of something else, sir. We've checked with the homeless shelters but what about the transition houses, soup kitchens, that sort of thing? Maybe ask there about our mystery man. Could be he shows up now and then."

"All right, Rachel, you run them down."

~~~

Nothing left for Jack to do but ride his bicycle back home. He had cut over to Olivia Street and was passing the cemetery when he remembered hearing about a transitional house just the other side of Truman. He turned up Grinnell.

Detective Rachel Powers had parked her car and was about to get out when she saw a man dressed in shorts and a nice t-shirt ride up on a red bicycle and go into the same house she'd come to. He was average looking—scale slightly tipped toward the handsome side—tall and *coiffed*. They'd met before.

She watched as Jack knocked on the front door. A woman answered and he went inside with her. Ten minutes later he came out. She waited for him to leave and then went to the house herself.

"Good day, ma'am," she greeted, showing her ID. "I'm Detective Rachel Powers with KWPD. We're investigating a couple of recent deaths involving the homeless and I was hoping that you might be able to help. May I come in?"

"Why, certainly," the woman said. "My name's Mabel Durham. That's terrible about those poor people."

Mabel led her to a small parlor.

"Please, have a seat," she offered. "You're the second visitor I've had today. Fellow just left, in fact. I don't know how I can help you. We offer transitional housing. Our guests have jobs. Generally, they just need a place to stay until they are fully back on their feet. You probably ought to talk with the people at KOTS."

"Yes, ma'am, thank you. I've spoken with KOTS and they were very helpful. The reason I'm here is to ask if anyone ever comes around who, well, has no business for doing so. I know that sounds odd."

Mabel Durham wasn't sure what to say.

"Sometimes a guest might have a visitor, if that's what you mean. But it wouldn't be unusual. Family member or a friend. Is that any help?"

"Yes, ma'am," Powers said. "I guess what I meant would be a stranger."

"No, there wouldn't be anyone like that, I don't believe."

"Never?" Powers asked.

Mabel laughed.

"Well, the man who just came. Hadn't been here before. But I don't think there was anything suspicious about him. He said he had a job opening at his restaurant. Wanted to know if anyone might be interested."

"Did he leave his name?" Powers asked, although she knew.

"Oh, yes, Jack Hunter. He gave me his card. Like I said to you, I told Mr. Hunter that all of our guest have jobs but I'd keep his offer in mind."

A troubling thought occurred to Powers. Suppose the card was a fake? And this man wasn't the same Jack Hunter that Gleason claimed to know. Yet the person she met at KOTS had said he was a friend of Gleason. And now she'd just seen that same person at this house. Which only proved that the card was his and that he had an interest in the homeless. And to her way of thinking that made him a *person of interest*.

Was that a dumb idea? Her old commanding officer once told her that there was no such thing as a dumb idea. Until it was proven to be so.

She thanked Mabel Durham and hurried back to her car. He was on a bike. He couldn't have gotten that far away.

But crisscrossing as many blocks as she might, she could find no sign of a man on a red bicycle.

She drove back to the police station, hoping to find Gleason still there but he'd left for the day. Perhaps she would call him later and run her ideas about Hunter past him. Right now, she needed to see a man about a washing machine.

Chapter 13

Some good local talent was lined up for tonight at the Undrinkable Bar. Jack was toying with the idea of sitting in. He hadn't played his saxophone for a couple of weeks, though, and his chops were rusty. He'd have to run through some scales, do a little workout for an hour or so and get himself back on the perch.

He was going to the closet where he kept his horn when his cell phone rang. Caller ID told him it was Laura Dalton's number.

"Hey, what's up?" he answered.

"Up to my neck here," she said. "How are you doing?"

"Busy. Have some problems with the new place. Billy's on top of it. Felt a little strange being back in Key West at first but I'm settling in. You okay?"

"Other than we're shorthanded here, I'm fine. This may bring back bad memories but I thought you ought to know that Benny Spring is dead. He was the talent agent that led us to Leonard Hall. He apparently committed suicide."

Jack was silent for a moment while images of Pamela Ridenour and himself in happier times cropped up in his mind.

"I'm sorry," he said. "Does anyone know why he did it?"

"Hollywood Division is handling the case. He jumped from his office window. There was no note or anything. Francine Mason told me about it. She worked for him when she was a reserve officer at West LA. She's a regular officer now at Hollywood."

"Well, that is sad," Jack said. "Even though I didn't know him."

Now it was Dalton's turn to pause.

"Jack, there's another reason I called," she said.

Jack caught the seriousness in the tone of her voice.

"More bad news?" he asked.

"I need to ask you a question," she said. "I should've talked about this when you were here. Too chicken, I guess."

"We're talking now," Jack said. "Ask away."

"What are you hoping for with me? I mean, where do you see our relationship, friendship or whatever you want to call it...where do you see this thing going?"

This caught Jack by surprise.

"Well, I don't know exactly," he said. "I guess I hadn't thought about it all that much. Just let things work themselves out, find their own way."

"I'm not trying to pressure you, Jack. But I *have* thought about it. And you are right, things sometimes do work themselves out and find their own way. They have with me. I like you and will always consider you my friend. But it's never going to be any more than that. Yeah, I know there've been a couple of times we were close and they were lovely. I mean that, Jack."

"They were lovely for me, too," he said, sensing a trapdoor beneath his feet was about to open. "But I'm not sure I understand."

"In other words, Jack, I don't see us having a long-term relationship as lovers or anything like that. I'm not ready. And frankly, if we're both being honest, neither of us is really in love with the other. We just keep drifting along and there's a reason for that. You know that. I do want us to remain friends, however. Do you understand now?"

Jack understood that this was bad news following bad news. He didn't reply.

"Jack?"

"Let me catch my breath," he said. "That was quite a blow."

"I know. It's just time to accept where we are and come

to a resolution so we can get on with our lives. Can we still be friends, though? I'd like that."

"Of course we can. May I ask if there's someone else? I mean, that's fine and I'm happy for you. Is there?"

"No one else, Jack," she answered with a slight catch in her voice. "Just me and my cat."

"Then we'll be the best of friends, Laura."

He hung up. He wouldn't be sitting in with the band tonight at the Undrinkable Bar after all.

~~~

Rachel Powers went for a combination washer and dryer. The salesperson promised the machine would be delivered and set up the next day. On her way back to the car, she noticed the old Pontiac that she'd seen before parked in the same spot. She didn't pay it any further attention. Probably belonged to someone who worked at the center.

Her thoughts returned to the man claiming to be Jack Hunter. She wished she'd taken a picture of him with her phone at that house. Gleason could then settle the issue that he was who he said he was. Even so, that wouldn't mean that he wasn't also someone they should be looking at. Your next-door neighbor could be a serial killer.

The intriguing thing was Hunter's interest in the homeless. She wasn't sure she bought this altruistic bullshit of wanting to give them jobs. But she needed something more solid before going to Gleason. She would start with a little research on the subject.

She drove back to the police station.

~~~

Jack had gone for a walk after the phone call and now found himself at the Key West Bight. One couldn't be in a prettier place at this time of day. The sun, orange and low to the west, had turned the water's surface to glass while eastward the sky readied for the approaching night.

He passed several large yachts where cocktails were being enjoyed aboard. Astrid Kelly and her magnificent boat sailed in on a long-ago memory. That ridiculous fight he'd had aboard it with Carl Napier and ending with the two of them falling overboard. He wondered where she might be. Far away, he hoped, and gave a silent laugh.

He was almost to the Galleon Tiki Bar. Happy hour should be well underway. Should he join them? No, he'd better keep company with his miserable self.

Instead of continuing on, he did an about-face and went back up the boardwalk. Laura had been right, of course. He should've been the one to have said it first. Not out of male pride but because, yes, to be honest he had felt the same way. Taking another step along that honest line, he hadn't been able to fully commit to any woman since Pamela had died. He was still in love with her, simple as that.

What had caused their marriage to break apart? Nothing you could put a finger on. It happened the way it had begun. Flaring intensely like striking a match only to burn itself out. They met, fell madly in love, married, divorced.

Suppose they'd had children, would the divorce have happened? He couldn't say. What if he'd fought harder to save the marriage? He'd done what he could. But if he'd done better, she'd be alive today, right? That was a question only a fool would ask.

So why was he still in love with her? Because he was a fool.

~~~

Detective Powers was having great success with her research. People were so uptight today about cell phone privacy but never give the Internet a second thought.

So far she'd found out that Jack Hunter had been an advertising executive in Los Angeles and now ran a highly successful real estate business there.   He'd also been considered a prospect by the LAPD during the investigation of his ex-wife's homicide but was eventually cleared. And a nice photograph verified that he was indeed the Jack Hunter she herself was interested in at the moment.

That significant brush with the law had been the only mention of anything suspicious. Otherwise, Hunter appeared to be an upstanding citizen. Spotless. Served his country in the Gulf War even. She might look into that.

And here in Key West he was just a businessman with a couple of job openings to fill. Sounds reasonable enough. And it would be if it were not for the homeless angle. She can't get past that. Why would anyone want to hire a homeless person with a sketchy record at best, when there must be hundreds of genuinely qualified people available? That was a question needing to be convincingly answered.

She plodded on.

Old records turned up the robbery investigation at the Inedible Cafe. It went pretty much as Gleason had said, as far as she could determine. Nothing there to point a finger one way or the other at Jack Hunter. But still...

More and more this guy was looking promising.

Chapter 14

Jack woke up feeling amazingly good. He had spent most of the evening before just walking around Old Town sorting out things and wisely passing up his favorite haunts. Now this was a new day.

After a quick shower and shave, where the mirror hinted that it was time for a haircut, he'd dressed and jumped on his new scooter and sped to the Inedible Cafe. He arrived at the slack-tide between breakfast and lunch.

"Spinach omelet, huh?" Billy said, breaking a couple of eggs into the frying pan. "Thought you were supposed to eat raw spinach. Gets cooked in an omelet."

Jack had once had a low red cell blood count and his doctor had suggested adding raw spinach to his diet to bring the numbers up. He'd followed her orders ever since.

"It's okay, Billy. Just cook it rare."

Jack walked out of the kitchen and sat at a table near the window. A cigarette would taste good, he thought. But he'd quit again. This time he meant it, too.

Billy brought over his omelet.

"Cup of coffee, Jack?" he asked.

"Sure, why don't you have one with me?"

Billy grunted and went to get the coffee pot.

"Great omelet," Jack said when he'd returned. "Spinach's done just right."

Billy sighed and sat down at the table.

""What's up, man?" Jack asked. "You've been pissed off since I got back to town."

"I dunno," he said, "must be worrying 'bout Stella. You found us a new chef at the pound yet?"

"That's your job, Billy. And calling the homeless shelter

a pound is kind of cold, don't you think? Anyway, I'm not the one looking for a chef."

"Just didn't want us working at cross purpose, that's all."

A moment of silence passed between them.

"I've been giving some thought about my ideas concerning the homeless," he said. "And I don't think it's fair to be loading you down with them. Yeah, I do want to help a little but maybe it should be done in other ways."

Billy brightened at this.

"They can always use bedding out there," he said.

"Use what?"

"Sheets, blankets and things. I know one man who gave ten or twenty brand new sets of bedding to them. Fellow lives right down the street from me. All the time doing good deeds."

"Well, thank you, I'll look into that."

"Something else, too. You could work at the soup kitchen. Need a reference, have 'em call me. I'll say you were the best pots and pans washer we ever had, hee-hee."

"That's a hell of an idea, Billy. I could volunteer a day or two."

Billy took on a serious expression.

"Now, wait a minute, Jack. I was just kidding. You don't want to go messing around out there. Folks are being killed at that campsite. No place to be sticking your nose in."

~~~

Powers and Gleason were grabbing a quick lunch at a restaurant near the station.

"Got your new washer yet?" Gleason asked while perusing the menu he'd seen a thousand times.

"Promised for today," Powers told him. "Gave the neighbor a key. He can let the delivery guy in. What are you thinking of having?"

"Burger. I don't know why I bother looking at this damn

thing. I know it by heart. What about you?"

"The chicken salad sandwich sounds good."

"I hear it's locally caught," Gleason said, spotting a Key West chicken strutting by on the sidewalk.

Powers put down her menu as the waitress approached.

"You two ready to order?" she asked.

"Burger for me," Gleason said. "Medium-well with fries."

"Make it two," Powers smiled.

She shifted uncomfortably in her seat. A familiar pain wrenched her back.

"You okay, Rachel?"

"Fine, sir. I'd like to talk about your friend."

"Who's that?"

"Jack Hunter. How well do you know him? I mean, I'm not trying to get personal but there's just something curious going on I want to run by you."

Gleason leaned back in his chair.

"Shoot," he said.

"Well, as you know, I first met him at KOTS. He was there allegedly trying to fill some job openings. At least that's what he said. I thought that strange at the time but apparently that kind of behavior is not unusual with him, right? Anyway, I've seen him again leaving a transitional house. The lady there said he had some jobs for her people. Now here's the thing. Jack Hunter could fit the description Tyler Bain gave of the man who wanted to buy drugs from Scott Endress. Especially the coiffed hair remark. I admit it's pretty general but still."

"Go on," Gleason said.

"I was up half the night on the computer checking out Hunter and found that for one thing he'd been a person of interest in his wife's homicide. Did you know that?"

"Actually, I did," Gleason said. "Let me give you a little history about him. But first, if you're really thinking about

Hunter for these killings, the guy wasn't in town when the first three went down."

"You know that for a fact, sir?"

"I met him the night after Endress was discovered. Said he'd just gotten in that morning."

"Doesn't necessarily mean he was being truthful, sir. But you said you knew about his wife?"

Gleason explained how he'd first come to know Jack and then about his help later in solving a homicide in Key West that had become a cold case. He also told her about Detective Laura Dalton's role in the investigation and how he'd learned of her earlier involvement with Jack.

"Detective Dalton was vacationing in Key West and volunteered to assist us," he said. "She and Hunter had become friends after the LA thing for some odd reason."

"Let me get this straight, sir," Powers said. "Jack Hunter was a person of interest in a Los Angeles murder that this detective was investigating and the two of them became an item afterwards?"

Gleason laughed.

"I don't know if they were ever an item, as you're suggesting," he said. "But, yeah, that's the way it apparently happened. That was after they caught the guy who killed Hunter's wife."

"Must be some kind of Stockholm syndrome in reverse," Powers speculated. "Creepy, if you ask me."

"It gets better," Gleason said seriously. "Or worse. I worked with him later on another case here. This one was tough. I think it got to him more than it did to me."

Powers waited for him to explain but he stopped at that.

"The guy can be a pain in the ass, no getting around it," he said, "but I can't see him as a serial killer. It's just not in him."

"That's the thing about them, sir," she argued confidently. "They never look the part. Hunter was also in-country during the Gulf War. Might be some kind of PTSD going on here."

Gleason gave her a skeptical look.

"Post-traumatic stress disorder? I'd be surprised. Hunter keeps a pretty cool head."

"His unit took part in some pretty hairy situations, sir. I looked him up. Jack Hunter was decorated for valor. Actually, twice. He got a Bronze Star which was later upgraded to the Silver Star."

"Yeah, but you're talking paranoid behavior, all that pathological shit. I just don't see Hunter as being that type."

"Takes all kinds, sir. When I was at college, I did my thesis on serial killers. I also attended a couple of symposiums on the subject. They really don't fit a mold."

"Well, follow your hunch is all I can say. It's never over until it's over."

His cell phone chimed. He used the first bar of I *Shot the Sheriff* as a ring tone.

"Do you think that song is appropriate, sir?" Powers asked when he ended the call.

"Probably not," Gleason said quietly. "Let's get out of here, detective. There's a db in the Sears lot."

Chapter 15

Two KWPD cruisers and a Sheriffs car cordoned off an area to the rear of the parking lot. A small crowd of onlookers gathered nearby. Gleason and Powers pulled up in their unmarked.

"What do we have?" Gleason asked an officer.

"Dead woman in the back seat," he said, pointing at a car. "Could be homeless. Security man found her."

The automobile was an older Pontiac. Its rear door stood open.

"He know her?"

"Said she often parked in this space but would move around to keep everybody happy. He'd noticed the car had been here for awhile this time. Went to look inside and saw her."

"Who opened the door?" Gleason wanted to know.

"He did," the officer said. "But swears he didn't touch anything. Could tell she was dead and called us."

Powers squinted at the car.

"I remember seeing this vehicle before, sir," she said. "The day I came here about my washer. A lady was sitting in the driver's seat putting on makeup."

Gleason turned to the car.

"We smiled at each other," Powers added wistfully.

The two detectives walked over to the Pontiac. A woman's body leaned to one side in a twisted position on the rear seat. Gleason pulled on a pair of gloves and poked his head in for a better look. He immediately backed away.

"Don't let anyone else near this car," he ordered the officer.

"What is it, sir?" Powers asked in alarm.

"I think we might have a hazardous situation," he said. "I want this car removed with the body untouched and taken to the impound yard."

He pushed the rear door closed.

Powers was baffled.

"I don't understand," she said.

"Bitter almond. I could smell it all over the body. Could be cyanide poisoning. Got to get this thing out of here and to where we have better control."

He pulled out his phone and called the station.

~~~

The fire department's Rescue 1 had stood by while the Pontiac was being loaded onto the flatbed truck. That particular unit rolled out whenever there was an accident or incident involving rescue assistance or Hazmat service. Gleason and Powers followed the truck to the KWPD impound.

"I don't know how much cyanide has contaminated that car, or even if it is that, but we can't take a chance," Gleason said.

He was talking to Sonny Rico, who was putting on a Hazmat suit. Rico worked as a technician for the police department.

Protective equipment is rated from Level A Red Zone, offering the maximum safety when the danger is unknown, to Level D Green Zone when the contaminant is known and below harmful amounts. Level A was the full getup for protection, a suit designed to keep out everything, including air. It supplied its own. Level D dressed you in coveralls and gloves.

Rico opted for Level C Yellow Zone, which was a big step up from the bottom line and on the safe side for decontaminating victims.

"You might want to back off a little," Rico suggested. "The ride over probably cleared the air but you never know."

Gleason and Powers quickly walked to the other side of the room and Rico opened the rear door of the Pontiac.

Janice Irwin's body had shifted somewhat and now slumped down on the right side of the seat. Rico worked around it. Finding no further evidence of chemical contamination, he stepped back and pulled up his face shield.

"It's safe to remove the body, detectives," he called out.

~~~

Dr. Blake Hardy had Janice Irwin taken to the Lower Keys Medical Center for autopsy. Gleason asked for the results as soon as they became available. Hardy promised he'd do his best but these were busy times, as he was certain the detective could appreciate.

"The sandwich goes to the lab," Gleason ordered. "Tell them to be careful with it."

The techs had swept the car for evidence and dusted for prints. Nothing outstanding besides the half-eaten chicken salad sandwich, which had been safely sealed in a container. Plenty of fingerprints around and probably all belonging to the victim.

"You believe she was poisoned?" Powers asked. "Why'd anyone want to do such a thing? I mean, that's so bizarre."

"Right now, we're dealing only with a suspicious death," Gleason said. "But I'm pretty sure the lab will find cyanide in that sandwich and the autopsy will confirm the woman died from it. Suppose you could ask if she put the stuff in the thing herself. Now that *would* be bizarre."

"It seems like such an iffy way to murder someone," Powers said. "How did whoever gave her the sandwich know she would eat it? What if she didn't like chicken salad?"

"The woman was homeless," Gleason said. "She wasn't going to turn down a free meal."

"But why pick her?"

"I don't know," Gleason answered. "Why the others? Random choice? Bad luck of the draw? I'm halfway into believing your serial killer theory. Don't know what's driving him but it has to have something to do with the homeless."

"Does that mean you're ready to consider your friend as a possibility, sir?"

"I can't see Jack Hunter as being a suspect but at this point I'm willing to look at everyone and anything."

~ ~ ~

Jack wiped off the scooter with an old towel. There hadn't been a speck of dust on it but why not? He put on his helmet and fired up the motor. He was going to tour the island.

Nearing the eastern end, he remembered that the soup kitchen was somewhere in this area. Should be easy to find.

He was lost in no time. Getting back on Roosevelt, he stopped at a gas station. Fortunately, the attendant knew the address.

The kitchen was housed in a building on the other side of the Blue Bayou. Jack parked out front and went in.

Lunch was the only meal they served and that time had long passed. A man was wiping down a table in the dining room and Jack walked over to him.

"How you doing," he said. "Wonder if you could give me a little information about your organization?"

"Sure, what do you want to know?"

"My name is Jack Hunter. I have some restaurant experience and thought maybe I could help out here."

"We can always use a hand," the man smiled. "I'm Mike Galvin. I volunteer in the kitchen myself two days a week."

"That's admirable," Jack said. "You retired?"

"Yes and no," Mike laughed. "I'm a lawyer by profession. Was with a law firm up in the Tampa area but came down here a couple years ago. Never went back. But I do some occasional pro bono work. Just to keep my finger in it, you know."

"Sounds to me like you're working two good jobs," Jack said.

"Guess you could call it that," Mike smiled. "The person you ought to talk with is Sonja Lidman. She's in charge of the kitchen but I think she's gone for the day."

"How can I get in touch with her?"

"She lives in Sugar Loaf. Your best bet would be to stop by tomorrow around noon."

Jack left the soup kitchen to continue with his tour.

Chapter 16

SERIAL KILLER ON THE PROWL sprawled across the front page of the newspaper the next morning in letters so large it took two lines to squeeze them in. The following story hammered on the lack of progress in the investigation and raised an ugly, though unfair, question—was it because the victims were homeless and therefore not a top priority??

"Everyone's working on this starting right this minute," Jay Halderman pronounced. He and Gleason were in his office. Powers was running down Janice Irwin on her computer in the detective's room.

"What about other cases?" Gleason asked.

"This is number one priority, Earl. You're the lead man. Take whoever else you need. Just get the thing done before I'm eaten alive. The chief, the mayor, every damn councilman, I even got a call from the Miami paper, they're all on my ass wanting to know what the hell we are doing. Now, what've you got for me?"

Gleason had never seen his boss so upset. Sure, this was bad but he wondered if there wasn't more going on behind the scene. Well, he wasn't about to kick that hornets' nest.

"You remember Jack Hunter?" he said.

"Isn't he a friend of that LA detective, what was her name?"

"Laura Dalton. He also was involved with the Ranzoas."

"Oh, sure, those poor kids at the cemetery. I remember him, why do you ask?"

Gleason cleared his throat.

"Detective Powers believes he could be worth looking at in these homeless killings."

He paused before continuing. Halderman leaned back

in his chair.

"I don't believe there's anything to it," Gleason said, "but Rachel apparently has done quite a bit of study on serial killers and Hunter has come up on her radar."

"Is she sharing why she thinks this?" Halderman asked.

"It *is* weird, I have to admit," Gleason said, "but then, so is Jack Hunter. Anyway, she first ran into him at KOTS when she was there asking about Kirby and Endress. Seems Hunter was interesting in hiring a couple of their guests. Then, she next saw him leaving a transition house just as she arrived to question the den mother there. Woman told her that he'd asked her the same thing. She checked out Hunter and found among other things, his military record. Seems he was a hero of sorts in the Gulf. Powers suspects he might suffer from PTSD. Again, I don't believe Jack Hunter is involved in any of this but I'm not ready to turn down the slightest possibility at this point. The other thing in his favor is that I ran into him the other night and he said he'd just gotten in town. If that's true, then he's clear."

Halderman scribbled down something on a notepad.

"That's easily checked," he said. "But I like the PTSD angle. Lot of combat vets in Key West. I'm not saying that makes them suspects but look at these murders. We've got four of them if you want to include the shooting at Rest Beach. That's four homicides, each by a different method but with one common factor. Overkill in each instance. Like Powers was saying, a hell of a lot of anger shown. Plus, the victims were all homeless. I'd say that's targeting. Then there's this..."

"Excuse me for breaking in, boss," Gleason said, "but we haven't gotten the ME's report on the Irwin woman. Right now, it's just a suspicious death."

"What? You think she committed suicide by lacing her goddamn sandwich with some kind of poison? Cyanide I believe you said."

"Haven't gotten the lab report on that either. Sorry."

"Earl, then for a point of discussion at the present time, let's just consider it a fucking homicide, okay?"

Gleason nodded.

"Now, where was I? Oh, yeah, we have four separate murders, four different methods for each crime—gunshot, stabbing, bludgeoning, poison. And the thing that connects them is the victims were homeless. Looks to me someone has an issue with homelessness."

"I agree," Gleason said. "But there's one small difference in Janice Irwin. The first three involved suspected drug dealings. No sign of that having been an issue on this latest."

Halderman turned in his chair and looked out the window.

"Wonder if the winner of that one-way bus ticket is still in town?" he mused. "Tyler Bain, remember him?"

"I'll call KOTS," Gleason said. "Probably gone, though."

"See if you can find him. He gave a vague description of the guy wanting to buy drugs from Endress. Maybe a sketch artist can make something of it. Should've done that back then. Don't know what the hell we were thinking."

"I'm on it."

"Not much of a lead but it's better than nothing," Halderman said tight-lipped. "Let Powers continue with Hunter. Who knows, she might be on to something. But don't stop there. We can't afford to get caught chasing out tails."

~~~

He read the headline aloud once more, practically screaming this time.

"Serial Killer On The Prowl!"

There was no one to hear him. He was at his home. He yelled it again.

"Serial Killer On The Prowl!"

He clipped the article from the newspaper and put it into a portfolio along with the others that he had spread on the table. These he would save. There'd be nothing incriminating should anyone ever come across them. Just satisfying a curiosity, that's all. All easily explainable.

The other folder was a different matter. It contained a dossier on each victim. Intelligence he had gathered while they were still alive. Routines. Friends. Physical condition. He wouldn't take on some motherfucker in better shape than himself. Drug use was important. Actually, it was the whole point of this little operation.

And he would have stuck with that had not another great idea occurred. His methodology was designed to keep the cops off balance. Use a different weapon each time. And it was working beautifully, wasn't it? He had those poor bastards running around crazy trying to figure out what was going on with these drug deals that'd gone down the tube. Regular epidemic, the way these dumb-fuck dealers were knocking off each other. Cops didn't know whether to shit or go blind. He had them on the ropes for sure. That's when he'd thought, why not a change-up?

Enter mousy little Janice Irwin. No drug use. No dealing. No family. And a woman. Hey, he was equal opportunity and gender all the way.

It'd been easy getting the low down on her. He was pretty experienced by now. And she was such a needy little thing. He'd picked up on that from the beginning.

Pay the smallest bit of attention to these assholes and they were yours. All of them, down to the last, creatures of habit. And no one gave a shit about them.

Certainly not him, pal. Been there, done that.

~ ~ ~

"Sure you don't want to take it for a spin?" Jack teased Billy, who'd popped his head out the kitchen door when he heard the moped pull up.

Billy grinned and shook his head no.

"Hop on. We'll ride around the neighborhood."

"C'mon, Jack." Billy said, ignoring him and turning to go back inside. "I've got an idea about getting us that new chef."

The restaurant had about finished with the breakfast shift. Billy motioned for Jack to take a table.

"You ever been down to St. Thomas, Jack?"

"Nope. Hear it's nice, though."

"I got a cousin lives there. Derrick Bean. Knows how a fish ought to be done. See, that's the other thing I was thinking about."

"Not sure I got the first thing, Billy."

"Derrick's a cook is what I was talking about," Billy said, like he was explaining the obvious to an idiot. "The other thing is Stella by Starlight and I'll get to that part soon as I'm finished with this one."

Jack held up both hands, palms out.

"Take your time, Billy. Don't let me rush you."

Billy eyed Jack once more before continuing.

"The way I see it is Derrick comes up here and takes over Stella by Starlight."

Jack opened his mouth to say something about that but Billy ran over top of him.

"Boy learned from his auntie. Just like me. But here's the kicker, Jack. We make the restaurant strictly seafood and serve only local caught that day. Already have the best fisherman lined up. Got his own boat, too. Keep us in fresh fish every day, hee-hee."

Billy leaned back with an ear-to-ear smile.

"Yes, sir," he said. "Knew we'd lick that ol' problem with Stella. Just had to wheel your nose to the grindstone, that's all."

Billy's metaphors were often mixed and painful to imagine.

"Your cousin's done this before, run a restaurant, that is?" Jack asked.

"Ain't all that hard," Billy shrugged. "I'll be there while he gets his feet wet."

Jack bit his lower lip and nodded.

"When's all this going to happen?"

"Sparrow Lovewell's meeting the jet plane this afternoon and bringing him down. That's one more thing, Jack. Be a big help if you could put up the boy until I find him a place."

"You mean stay with me?"

"I'd keep him myself 'cept my house is a mess with all that new painting going on. Thought you could let him have that little room you got out back. Shouldn't be for long."

"Sure," Jack sighed. "Ask Sparrow to call me when they hit town."

~~~

Tyler Bain had a ticket to ride on the next morning's bus. He was spending his last sunny day in Key West hanging out at KOTS and catching a few rays on the bench to pass the time. He'd earlier phoned an uncle in Hattiesburg who'd promised to give him a room. He was looking forward to going back home. Well, it beat living on the street—at least he'd have a real roof over his head there. Getting the hell out of here was the best thing. But his day quickly darkened, as if the sun had slipped behind a cloud when he saw Detective Powers pull up in front. His instinct was to jump up and run but instead he merely waved her a little greeting.

"Hello, Tyler," she said, getting out of her car. "Things going all right?"

"Yeah, going great. Like I'm going away from this hole tomorrow."

"Well, I wish you the best of luck, Tyler but I'm glad to have run into you before you go. That man you mentioned wanting to buy drugs when we last talked. I wonder if you'd help us get a better description of him."

Tyler hesitated.

"Why should I help you?" he said.

"Because it's the right thing to do, Tyler. You're about to start a new life."

She opened the backseat door and motioned for him to get in.

Chapter 17

"Homicide, this is Detective Dalton," she answered, grabbing up the phone and setting down a cup of coffee on her desk.

She'd just walked into the detective's room at Van Nuys and all the phones were going crazy. The other detectives hadn't arrived yet.

"Good morning, Laura," a familiar gruff voice replied. "Didn't expect to find you there so early."

She smiled broadly.

"Detective Hagen," she said.

Hagen had been her Detective Three and mentor in West Los Angeles when they both worked homicide. He'd since retired.

"Early bird catches the worms. How's the mule business?"

After retiring he and his wife had moved to a ranch in Arroyo Grande and started raising mules. He soon became the go-to person for anyone wanting to buy a mule. Horse trading belonged to a neighbor the next ranch over. Hagen credited his success with mules to the thirty years of experience he'd gained working with the LAPD.

"Keeping us in hay," he laughed, then got down to the subject. "The reason I'm calling, Laura, is there's something you might be interested in knowing. Leonard Hall has been released."

She audibly gasped. This was shocking! They'd turned the little killer loose?

"My God, I don't know what to say. When did this happen?"

"Haven't got the exact date. You can't expect the prison

to notify the department every time an asshole is paroled or what. Beverly has a sister who lives in Coalinga. Her hubby's a guard at Pleasant Valley State Prison. Whenever we visited with them, he'd always want to talk about the Ridenour case. Apparently, Hall was on his cellblock and for some reason he was fascinated about how we finally caught the bastard. So he called here to let me know what'd happened."

Dalton still couldn't quite fully take it in.

"Do you know how it came about?" she asked.

"Technicality from what I gather. Some kind of foul-up with the judge at the trial. You remember Hall had a real sharpie for a lawyer. Guess he found a crack somewhere and these days that's all it takes."

"That case was solid," she said angrily. "What's the DA going to do? Retry him, I hope."

Hagen took in a breath.

"No joy there either, Laura. My understanding is he's going to take a pass. Probably too expensive for a retrial. Everybody's so damn budget-conscious. Besides, Hall would be eligible for parole in another year or so. Cheaper to get rid of him now and make room for the next one."

"But this guy flat out murdered someone," she protested. "He's not any small-time hoodlum. And what? After serving...is it three years? Yeah, three damn years and he walks. Says a lot for the system, huh?"

"Like you said a minute ago, Laura, our job's just to catch the worms. What the court does with them is its business."

A couple of detectives came into the room, noisily laughing. She stuck a finger in her free ear to block them out.

"Are you still in touch with Jack Hunter?" Hagen asked.

She blushed and mentally kicked herself for doing it. Why had that embarrassed her? They'd reached a rapprochement, hadn't they? Move on, girl.

"He's in Key West. I don't see him often."

"Well, that's probably a good thing," Hagen said. "Might be a shade upset about his wife's murderer getting out of jail—could try something rash if he were still here. Well, you take care, Laura. Give me a call sometime or better yet, come for a visit. We can go mule riding."

She thanked Hagen and said she might take him up on that offer, knowing full well she had no intention of ever placing a foot or bottom, as it were, on any mule. After they'd hung up, she wondered if she should have mentioned Benny Spring's suicide. But then, why? Had nothing to do with Hall's release. She let it drop.

On second thought, however, she would call Francine Mason to tell her the news.

~~~

Leonard was presently staying in a sleazy motel on Van Nuys Boulevard where rooms went by the hour, day, or week. Huge comedown from an earlier time before his life had been dumped on. He'd dwelled on that for three long years.

It wasn't fair. He had been a talent waiting to be discovered. Hanging out in the hot spots. Had a script ready and begging to be bought. Just needed the right person to get behind it. So what happened?

Jack Hunter happened.

He'd been Jack's secretary at the ad agency, a fill-in job until he hit the big time. He had approached Jack with his script, offering him a piece of the action if he'd pony up a little money for production, but the guy had no foresight. Of course, he lacked the talent to write anything himself. Probably jealous of those who could, too. Just another ad agency hack marking time until he got his gold watch.

But Jack's wife was different. Pamela was a sharp lady. And she had the two things he needed. Money and heavy

Hollywood connections.

It could've been so good but Jack would have none of it. That was obvious when he showed Pamela the script. Her husband had already poisoned her about it and him.

Well, she paid. And now Benny Spring had as well. So why shouldn't Jack Hunter? He's the reason he's living at this flophouse instead of in Beverly Hills. He wondered where Hunter lived.

He went into the office to use the phone.

"The Palmer Agency," a pleasant-sounding woman's voice announced. "This is Brenda, how may I help you?"

Brenda Carson was a friend of Jack Hunter's. He'd gotten her the receptionist job with his company after her former boss at a classic car-finding service had been murdered and the business closed.

"Hello Brenda, is Jack Hunter there?" Leonard asked, matching her friendly tone.

"Mr. Hunter is out of the office," Brenda said primly. "May I ask who's calling?"

"Oh, gee, that's too bad. Do you know when he might be back?"

"I couldn't say."

"Just tell him Bill Evans called, would you? We served together in Iraq and I'm just in town for the day. Wanted to catch up with him about old times."

Leonard had pulled that name out of the air. He didn't want to tip off Jack that he was back. He had known Jack had once served somewhere in the military. It worked, too. Brenda felt a pang of sympathy.

"Oh, I'm so sorry. Actually, Jack is in Florida. I'll certainly tell him you called. I know he'll be sad to have missed you."

Brenda immediately realized she shouldn't have mentioned Florida.

"Florida? You wouldn't happen to know where, would

you? I'm retired and my wife and I live in, uh, Miami. Heading back now."

She knew she shouldn't say but she did.

"He's in Key West."

"I don't suppose you have a number where I could reach him?"

She did it again.

~~~

Gleason had sloughed off the sketch artist job to Powers. Now she and Tyler Bain huddled in an interview room at the police station while the artist finished the drawing.

"Everybody happy?" the artist asked, holding up his work. "The norm today in law enforcement is to use a computer to make these drawings. Much broader base to build from. Faster, too. And mucho cheaper. Don't often use pencil and paper. But we didn't seem to have a whole lot to go on here. Computer would've probably just ginned up a white-bread male you'd find in a picture frame at the store. An artist, though, can draw anything."

Rachel Powers was disappointed by what this artist had drawn, however. She'd been expecting to see Jack Hunter looking back at her. Not an unremarkable face that could belong to anyone. Say in a picture frame.

"How about it, Tyler?" she asked, hoping he could add some positive detail.

Tyler squinted for a moment, then leaned forward for a closer examination. Powers halfway expected him to hold up his thumb next to measure the perspective.

"Think so," he finally said. "I didn't pay much attention to him that night."

"What about the hair?" Powers prompted. "You remembered that he had a nice haircut. Does this style fit him?"

"Yeah…guess so," Tyler shrugged. "Seems about right.

Like I said, I didn't pay all that much attention."

    "Coif up the hair a little more," Powers told the artist.

    The artist made a few pencil flourishes.

    Powers turned to Tyler.

    "Well?" she said.

    "Yeah, that's him. Kinda."

Chapter 18

Jack awoke to loud knocking on his front door. He glanced at the bedside clock. One a.m.

"Jack! It's Sparrow. You asleep?"

He sat up, gathered his wits and threw his feet to the floor."

"Jesus Christ, Sparrow, it's one o'clock in the morning!" he called out. "Hold on, I'm coming."

He turned on the porch light, peeked out the window, and saw two men standing there. Sparrow and another he didn't recognize wearing a silvery-toned suit that made him resemble an industrial freezer. He opened the door for them.

"Didn't think you were sleeping," Sparrow laughed. "Saw the light on over there and figured you hadn't gone to bed yet."

Jack always left on a table lamp in the front room ever since he'd been shot by someone lying in wait one night long ago.

"You were supposed to call me when you got to town," Jack said irritatedly. "What happened?"

"Plane was late," Sparrow explained. "Didn't get any supper so we stopped at a restaurant in Homestead. Got there just before they closed. Wasn't that lucky? Oh, this is Derrick Bean."

Derrick smiled broadly and stuck out his hand. A catcher's mitt.

"Pleased to meet you, Mr. Hunter," he said in a clipped British accent. "Thank you for letting me stay here. I hope this doesn't inconvenience you."

"No problem," Jack said.

"You wouldn't have a cold beer in the refrigerator, would you, Jack?" Sparrow asked. "Long drive down the Keys."

Two hours and a couple of six-packs later, Derrick had been shown to his room, Sparrow sent on his way home and Jack, now collapsed in bed, awaited for sleep lost and never to return.

~~~

"The medical lab report on Janice Irwin came in," Gleason told Powers. "Cyanide poisoning. Humungous amount."

The two detectives were at their desks readying for the day ahead. Gleason took a sip of coffee grown cold and made a face.

"Christ, this stuff is awful," he said. "Something must be wrong with that damn machine."

"Would you like a fresh cup, sir?" Powers asked. "I was just about to get one for myself."

"Thanks, but I'd rather get on with this report. The cyanide is curious. Hard to come by. Not something you can pick up at the drugstore."

"What about pesticides?" Powers suggested. "Isn't it used in rat poison?"

"No, I've looked into several sources. One outfit sells a bait for predators that uses cyanide but you can't buy it here. Too dangerous. It's also used in metal preparation or some strange crap like that. Still not available to just anyone. We should keep checking, though."

Powers got up and went to the coffee machine. She brought back two cups.

"You know, Saddam Hussein used that in the eighties against the Kurds," she said. "Committed genocide."

"Yeah, but that was cyanide gas. Kill you just as fast. But here we have cyanide crystals put in a sandwich by some maniac to murder a homeless woman. What the hell?"

Powers though for a moment.

"Is there any connection to the methods used in the cases, I wonder? Gun, knife, bludgeon and now poison. Some kind of order that we're missing?"

"I can't see any logic in their order," Gleason said. "The best answer is that this is some kind of a sick game and the way he kills is part of it. We've gone over all this before, Rachel."

Powers picked up a copy of the sketch artist composite from a stack on the desk. She examined for a half minute, shrugged her shoulders and put it back.

"Could be anybody," she sighed. "I have to tell you I was pulling for it to be your friend, Jack Hunter."

"I appreciate your determination, detective," Gleason said, "but I repeat, I never figured Hunter for this. Pain in the ass? Number one on the list."

Powers blushed.

"The bag the sandwich came in, sir," she said. "Plain like you'd buy at the supermarket. Why would she accept it from a stranger? Yeah, she was homeless but didn't seem to be down and out. She even had some money in her purse."

Gleason thought about this.

"People often give food to the homeless," he said. "Nothing really suspicious about that. And our victim didn't know how long that money would last. It's the modus operandi that's so frustrating in this whole damn business. We know what happened in each homicide but not why? Yeah, yeah, the killer obviously has something against homeless people. We think. Or does he? Maybe it's a thrill killer."

"Could there be more than one, sir? You said a thrill killer. What if there were two or even three? Some kind of kill-for-thrill club. That's not far-fetched. Wouldn't be the first time, either."

Gleason stared at her.

97

"That's a possibility," he said. "But my gut tells me it's just one person. We'll release the sketch to the newspaper. That's the best we've got for now. We really need the public's help."

~~~

A marvelous thought had occurred to Leonard after he'd hung up from talking with Brenda Carson. He made another phone call to his and Jack's old advertising agency, Gaysome Hoigh, in Santa Monica. There he discovered that not only was William Wardel still with the company—he'd been another arrogant jerk who had passed on investing in the screenplay—he was now its damn president! Of course, the big man was too busy to take his call—he'd given the secretary there a false name this time— but that wasn't the purpose of his phoning the agency. Leonard knew Wardel parked in the building's underground space. He always kept a spare ignition key in a little box stuck with a magnet in the left front wheel well.

~~~

Jack had called a taxi for Derrick. The man was simply too big to fit on the back of the scooter. He followed the cab to the Inedible Cafe. Billy was standing out front when they pulled up.

"Hey, Derrick," he shouted. "Come give your 'ol cousin a hug, hee-hee."

Derrick draped his arms around Billy, almost making him disappear in their fold.

"Go on inside," he gasped upon being released. "Got to talk to Jack for a minute."

Derrick went in and Billy grinned mightily.

"Boy's something, all right. Just wanted to thank you for putting him up. Won't be long 'fore he can stay with me."

"Oh, don't worry about that, Billy. Take your time."

Jack then gave Billy a sly look.

"Derrick learned to cook from his momma, huh?"

Billy narrowed his eyes.

"Sure, Jack, just as same as me, hee-hee."

Jack laughed, too.

"So you're saying she taught both of you at the Cordon Bleu," he said. "That right?"

Billy said nothing in return.

"We were talking this morning and Derrick told me that he'd spent two years at the school in France and afterwards another four years as an assistant chef in some fancy restaurant in London. Probably where he picked up that English accent, huh?"

"People talk like that in the islands," Billy said seriously. "Got the British Virgins down there. Sure, I knew the boy had some experience. Wouldn't have asked him to come up here if I didn't think he could handle the job."

"Hey, man, I think it's fine," Jack said. "Just can't understand why anyone with *that* kind of experience would want to come here, that's all."

"Family, Jack."

And Jack had no problem with that either.

"Well, he seems like a pretty good guy to me," he yawned. "Sorry, late night. I'm going to leave you two and go get a haircut."

~~~

"Lieutenant, there's a reporter from a Miami television station out front wanting to talk with someone about the Blue Bayou homicides," the desk officer reported.

"Have public affairs handle it," Halderman said, sharply.

"No one's in. Including the captain."

"Damn. All right, all right, I'll see him," Halderman grumbled, getting up and following the officer.

A flashy-looking blonde woman and a young man stood waiting at the desk.

"I'm Lieutenant Jay Halderman. How can I help you?"

"My name's Gina Rivera," the woman said smartly, thrusting out her hand. "I'm with WPIS evening news and would like to ask you some questions about the serial murders. Why are the homeless being targeted? Do you have a suspect?"

"We aren't investigating a serial killer," Halderman told her, ignoring the proffered hand. "If you're talking about the recent homeless homicides, we're regarding them as separate incidents at the present."

The woman snorted a haughty laugh.

"Really? The local newspaper says they're the work of a serial killer. Plastered right across the front page. Seems the so-called Blue Bayou has become a killing field."

She held up a copy of the paper.

"C'mon, Lieutenant, you've got four unsolved murders," she pressed on. "All the victims were homeless. I'd say there's a lunatic on the loose in Key West who has a real problem with the homeless. What are you doing about it?"

Halderman had reached the limit of his patience with this pushy woman.

"You really need to talk with our public affairs officer," he said firmly. "I can't give you any information concerning an ongoing case. Good day, ma'am."

Gina Rivera hadn't come to this godless place for nothing. She tacked to a different course. She'd make nice to this stiff.

"I understand your situation, Lieutenant," she purred. "We'll try to make an appointment with your PA officer. It's just that we drove down early this morning. Traffic was unbelievable, as you can imagine. And I have to leave soon to get back in time for my show. Let me ask you this one tiny thing. As I said, I can certainly see why you're hesitant to mention anything about a serial killer. Could cause a panic. But do you have anything you could give me? Has anyone come forward? A witness? Maybe we could be a help to get the word out. We *do* have a wide audience."

Halderman thought about the artist's sketch. Patrol already had copies. And the paper would be running it tomorrow. Wouldn't hurt to give her one, but he'd play it down. Not that there was much to begin with.

"Excuse me," he said. "I'll be right back."

"This drawing was based on a vague description given by an unreliable source of a man who was seen near the Blue Bayou at the time of one murder," he said, returning with a copy of the sketch.

~~~

Jack relaxed in a chair on the rear deck of Jewel Bank's boat docked in Garrison Bight. Her boat was a live-aboard 38-footer that rarely saw open water. It was a member of the tight little houseboat community. A number of musicians lived here and Jack had sat in with a few of them at the Undrinkable Bar.

"Just a little off the sides," he said to Jewel.

Jewel was a barber who worked from home and had a decent trade. Both men and women. She was also a bassist with the Flamin' Flamingos, a girl rock band that played the lower Keys. Bookings for the band had become scarce lately but the barbering remained steady.

"Haven't seen you for awhile, Jack," she said while stropping a straight razor. Jewel specialized in razor cuts.

"Been out of town. Los Angeles."

"I love LA."

"Think someone has already written that."

A pelican made a low pass across the stern, banked hard to starboard, and flared to land on a nearby piling.

"Know who I heard from and who might be moving back to town? Ruby Steele."

Jack turned his head at that and caused Jewel to slice off a tuff of hair.

"Now look what you made me do!" she said. "Could've been your ear. I'll have to even up the other side."

Jack had known Ruby Steele during his first stay in Key West. She'd been a rocker in Miami before coming to the island and founding the Church of a Joyful Noise. Her ex-boyfriend drug dealer had shown up and Jack, with the best of intentions, had intervened on her behalf. No good came of it and Ruby, fearing for her life, left town in a hurry.

"That's terrific,' he said. "Did she say when?"

"Just that she was thinking about it."

"Well, if you hear back, please tell her to call me."

"I'm not sure she'd be all that happy but I'll tell her anyway."

Jewel picked up a mirror and showed Jack his new haircut.

"Like it?"

"Not too coifed is it?"

Chapter 19

A new flatscreen television set had been installed earlier that day in the bar at the Inedible Cafe. It hung in a corner close to the ceiling and angled down so it could easily be seen. Billy and Jack flicked through the channels.

"Man, the programming down here sucks," Jack complained. "Maybe we don't need television. The Undrinkable isn't a sports bar."

"Got twenty-nine channels, Jack. Find something good."

"Friend of mine has an all-girl rock band," Jack said. "Flamin' Flamingos. We ought to hire them for a couple of nights. Draw a bigger crowd than this thing."

"Hush, Jack. There's the news."

The WPIS music fanfare died and the commentator, squaring off a stack of papers in front of him, announced the leadoff story.

"Serial killer on the loose in Key West." he stated gravely. "Our own Gina Rivera has the details."

Gina's serious face filled the screen.

"This is Gina Rivera reporting for WPIS from the so-called Blue Bayou, a homeless encampment in Key West."

The camera pulled back to reveal her standing on a bank overlooking a small body of water.

"Across from here in those mangroves," she gestured, "two homeless men were brutally murdered. A homeless woman was recently found dead in her car not far from this location. And an earlier fatal shooting involving another homeless man occurred less than two miles away. Is this the work of a serial killer?"

The scene changed to a closeup of the mangroves as she

continued.

"The Blue Bayou, a no-man's land populated by the forsaken with little to lose. And where death now stalks these unfortunates. What must it be like to spend a night in there?"

The picture returned to her.

"So far the police seem to be at a standstill in the investigation. However, WPIS has obtained a sketch of a possible suspect in these horrific crimes."

Gina held the drawing while the camera zoomed in for a close-up.

"Do you know this man?" she asked. "Have you seen anyone resembling him?"

Billy turned to Jack with a puzzled expression.

"Something familiar about that guy," he said.

~~~

This was the funniest thing he'd ever seen. Hilarious! Did they actually expect anyone to identify him from that? A blind man could've drawn a better likeness. Although he did love the big hair.

He fingered the small, gold charm on a string tied around his neck after the newscast had moved to another topic.

That police sketch was something to think about. Someone had to have given a description, no matter how sketchy...so someone must have noticed him. Sketchy, ha! He liked his sense of humor. But seriously, he couldn't just ignore the stupid drawing.

He went to the bathroom and studied himself in the mirror.

~~~

Another homicide had been called in right after Detective Dalton's conversation with her old boss. Getting back to Francine Mason in Hollywood with the news of Leonard Hall being released from prison had completely slipped her mind. Days later and at home one evening, she remembered. It was old news now. She called anyway.

"Francine, this is Laura Dalton. Hope I'm not disturbing you."

"You just caught me on my way out. Got a hot date, ha, ha."

Dalton wondered what one of those would be like. God, it'd been so long since she'd seen anyone.

"I won't keep you," she said. "Thought you ought to know that Leonard Hall's no longer in prison. Some technicality about the judge's instruction to the jury."

"That's terrible. But how could they have done that? Leonard was crazy. Some kind of sociopath or worse. He should've at least been sent to a psychiatric hospital. When was he released?"

"Don't know exactly. Hagen told me."

"I was curious because of what happened to Benny Spring," Mason said.

"Oh? Now that's kind of interesting. Tell me."

"Not that he had anything to do with Benny jumping out the window. Maybe I'm just tying the two together because of my being at Benny's when Leonard was there. He was a scary person. You didn't see it at first, but, boy, could it come out. I know that Benny made a big deal over that inane script that Leonard wrote and promised him the moon."

"That script cooked Hall's goose," Dalton said. "Practically followed in the murderer's footsteps."

"Yeah, and talk about karma, Benny later sold the thing for a ton. I don't know if Leonard ever saw any of it. They didn't have a contract."

Something rustled in a dark corner of Dalton's mind. But didn't show itself.

"Who's working this?" she asked.

"Lugo Croaker. He's a detective two."

The mention of the name caused Dalton to pause. She felt a sudden panic.

"Is he new with Hollywood?" she asked tentatively.

She hadn't thought about Lugo Croaker for years. Since they'd both left the police academy. Actually, she'd tried to forget him. And thought she had until now.

"He came up from Southwest."

Southwest LA going toward Compton was one of the toughest divisions in Los Angeles. As a cop you either loved it or considered it a penal camp.

"I'd told him that I had known Benny. He didn't seem to be all that interested."

"Thanks, Francine. I'll give him a call later."

"He's kind of a Neanderthal. At least, that's the word on him from the women at Southwest."

"Work with cavemen every day," Dalton said. "Have fun on your hot date."

Francine laughed and said she was taking her brother and his wife to the At, a popular restaurant with a neon @ out front. They were visiting from Bodega Bay, a little town more than five hundred miles north of LA.

After they'd hung up, Dalton jotted down some notes. She put Croaker out of her mind and concentrated on Leonard Hall's trial and his behavior during it. He'd been dressed in a solid-citizen suit and given a conservative haircut. He was the picture of innocence during opening statements but as the trial progressed and the prosecution chipped away, the inner Leonard began to reveal itself. Arrogance, disinterest, the occasional smirk, even winked at one of the jurors. During her testimony, however, he'd remained sullen. And under cross-examination by the defense, he'd glared at her with unbridled hatred.

Jack Hunter was there as a spectator. The State didn't need him as a witness and the defense tried to have him removed, contending his presence would prejudice the jury, but the judge ruled that he could stay. Leonard turned around to look at him a couple of times and grinned. Jack bore through it stoically. She thought that must have been an ordeal for him. In his shoes, she would've wanted to smash the bastard in the face. That was the beginning of their odd friendship-slash-relationship.

The jury returned a guilty verdict after four hours of deliberation. Leonard jumped to his feet, screaming angrily at them and then to Jack, threatening that this wasn't over. The bailiffs carried him out of the court room.

First thing in the morning she would call Pleasant Valley State Prison and find out exactly when Leonard Hall had been released. She'd deal with the Neanderthal later.

Chapter 20

"**T**his is our lucky day," Sonja Lidman said sarcastically. "One of our volunteers has called in sick. Must be something going around. Always is, isn't?"

Sonja ran the kitchen. She was a middle-aged woman with a kind face and a generally good disposition. She lived in a tiny house on Sugar Loaf Key with three cats, one dog and a disabled husband. Their two sons were in the Navy aboard a destroyer deployed in the South China Sea. Her pay from the charity foundation that supported the kitchen helped to shore up their income.

"Could you come in today?" she asked. "I know that's short notice but we expect a big crowd. It's barbecue day."

"Not a problem," Jack responded. "Like you said, your loss is my gain. What time?"

"Soon as you can get here."

Jack had been hanging around his house taking care of a few chores. The last one was trying to repair a dripping faucet in the bathroom that'd now upgraded itself to a job for the plumber. He cleaned up and hopped on his scooter.

The kitchen was only a fifteen-minute ride away and he pulled up to find a line already formed outside. A woman stood at an outdoor barbecue. He walked over to her.

"Are you Sonja?" he asked. "I'm Jack Hunter."

"Thank God you're here," the woman said, removing an apron tied around her waist and handing it to Jack. "We're doing hamburgers and hotdogs. No chicken. Buns and rolls are on the table over there. Same for mustard, ketchup and chopped onions. Cook everything medium—try not to burn too many. Supply's limited."

Four people were waiting in line with hotdog rolls in

hand. Jack tied on the apron and grabbed a pair of tongs.

"Getcher red-hot dogs here!" he shouted.

It was late afternoon by the time the barbecue was over and Jack had cleaned the grill, mopped the kitchen floor, and wiped down the stainless steel counters. Sonja Lidman walked in as he was finishing.

"You're a good worker," she said, looking around the room. "You've done this before?"

"I was once the chief bottle washer at a local restaurant," he laughed.

"Well, I certainly appreciate your help. Don't suppose I could get you back tomorrow? It's pasta day. Much easier."

Jack thought about that for a moment.

"Who could resist pasta day," he said. "Same time?"

"That'd be perfect. Mike Galvin is our regular volunteer but as I told you when you called, he's out sick. Hopefully, he'll be back soon."

"Happy to be of service," Jack said. "I think I talked with Mike. Do you have other people to come in?"

"We did until all these murders started happening. Now everybody's scared to even be near the homeless. It's sad. Mike's the only one who's stuck around."

"Well, you can count on me until he returns for duty."

~~~

Unappealing didn't come close to describing how Rachel Powers felt about driving up to Miami. She'd made the drive before and it was five hours of boredom. But there was no avoiding this trip, the old war wounds had decided enough was enough. She needed to see the doctors at the VA hospital. Maybe more than one. The memories were as bad as the pain.

He'd raced toward them on a motorcycle. There had been a sergeant, two other enlisted men, herself and a major who'd just arrived and was being shown around. The area had been declared safe.

The sergeant, for some reason his name escapes her to this day, first spotted the fast-approaching cycle. He yelled a warning. And she threw herself against the major, knocking both of them to the ground and shielding his body with hers. The terrorist's suicide vest exploded ten feet from the group, immediately killing the sergeant and the two soldiers. Shrapnel tore into her back and legs. The major was uninjured.

Months later she was awarded the Bronze Star and Purple Heart and released from the hospital with severe scarring on her legs and recurring pain radiating along her spine. Several operations reduced the scarring to the point of being hardly noticeable. Medication helped relieve the pain but dependence on drugs of any type went against her nature. So she'd decided to kick the habit. She'd always taken pride in her ability to persevere but now it was time to swallow her pride and perhaps some good meds as well.

"Sir, I have an appointment at the VA hospital in Miami tomorrow morning," she told Gleason. The two of them were at the homicide desk. It was late afternoon.

"Are you okay?" Gleason asked.

"Nothing serious," she said. "I should be back by the end of the day."

"When are you leaving?"

"Thought I'd get away before daybreak."

"Now might be better. Have a relaxing dinner. Get a good night's sleep. I know a nice motel close to the hospital. Hang on and I'll give 'em a call."

"Outstanding, sir."

~~~

The two youths couldn't believe their eyes. A new Lexus with the keys left in the ignition? Parked in this Phoenix neighborhood? Had to be a trap. Cops did things like that. Set up a bogus vehicle just begging to be taken and as soon as you drove off in the damn car, the engine quit and the doors locked. Then they had your ass. Still.

They walked past the Lexus and stopped at the corner to look back. The street was empty. They came up with a plan.

The younger one was underage and had no record. He'd take the car. The older one would wait for him in the next block. If he made it that far.

Less than five minutes later the pair of them were laughing as they headed for Interstate 10 and Nogales where this baby would soon be on its way to a new owner in Mexico City.

In Santa Monica, William Wardel had just finished filing a stolen car report with the Santa Monica police department.

~~~

Derrick Bean had long ago left for the restaurant by the time Jack got home from the soup kitchen.

So far, Billy's cousin was working out well at Stella by Starlight. Jack had recently eaten there, actually had the fish special, and it wasn't bad. Simply prepared like a fish should be. He hadn't mentioned that to Billy—maybe he should

Tonight, however, he wasn't up for a big meal. The afternoon of hot dogs and hamburgers had dulled any appetite he might've had. He showered and got dressed in a fresh t-shirt and shorts. That seemed to be all he wore lately. And to think he used to be a real clotheshorse. Well, that's Key West for you.

It was still light and he decided that a stroll over to Vinos for a glass of merlot would cap the day. He walked along Angela past the cemetery and then moved like a chess piece, criss-crossing the blocks and coming out on Duval Street just steps away from the wine bar.

Gleason sat at a table on the porch.

"I'm about to leave," he said as Jack came up the steps.

"You still have half a glass of wine," Jack noticed, sitting down. "What's the big rush?"

"Present company."

"Try not to always be a jerk, detective," Jack smiled. "You're better than that."

"See the paper today?" Gleason asked, handing a copy he'd been perusing to Jack.

"Yeah, seems like you aren't making much headway with these murders."

"You'd be surprised but actually I meant the article about the turkey attack. It's on the back page."

Jack gave him a concerned look.

"Someone attacked Turkey?" he said, turning to the page. "And they stuck it on the back? Who was it, ISIS?"

"It was wild turkeys," Gleason told him.

"Thought there were only chickens down here," Jack laughed, putting down the newspaper.

"Happened in New Jersey," Gleason said. "Bunch of wild turkeys ganged up on a mailman and chased him back to his truck. Guy had to hide inside until the police came and shooed them away."

Jack laughed again.

"What's the punch line?"

"Not one," Gleason shrugged. "Just a story in the newspaper. Kind of interesting, though."

"Why is that?"

"Wild turkeys were all but gone in New Jersey and now it looks like they've made a comeback."

Both men remained silent for a moment.

"Well, I suppose that's good news for the turkeys," Jack said. "Tells me something else I never realized, too."

"And?"

"You're a funny guy."

"Sometimes. But mostly I'm a serious guy. Nothing like Detective Powers however. Now there's a serious woman.

You want to know how serious she is. She's dead-set on you being behind these homeless homicides. And here's where it gets even more serious—I'm starting to think she might be on to something."

Gleason stared at Jack with a flat expression.

Jack heaved a breath, his eyebrows raised.

"Like I said, I never realized you had a sense of humor until now."

"It's not a joke, Hunter. All things considered, you're the best we've got."

"Then I suggest you and Detective Powers either put up or shut up."

Gleason finished his glass of wine and stood.

"See you around," he said.

Jack watched as the detective blended into the sidewalk traffic. Then he turned his attention back to the newspaper Gleason had given him. On the second page was a story about the homicides and a drawing of a person wanted for questioning. The sketch looked nothing like him, even by the wildest stretch of imagination. A nondescript face capped with longish hair.

He unconsciously touched his own hair.

What could have Powers running around in a dither over him? he wondered. And what was it about her that he'd sensed when they met at KOTS? Interesting woman. He might even pay her a call.

~~~

Gleason nuked half of a leftover pizza in the microwave and uncorked a bottle of merlot. Mitts rubbed against his legs, meowing for his own dinner.

"Keep it down, will you? I'm working as fast as I can."

He opened the refrigerator and took out a can of cat food. The meowing morphed into a rumbling purr and Mitts raced to the balcony door, tail straight up.

Day had swapped for night and Gleason lit a candle on

the small table outside. With the cat happily hunched over its food bowl, he poured himself a glass of wine and picked up a slice of pizza. Dvorak's 9th symphony swelled from inside.

His thoughts settled on the present homicide case. This whole business with Jack Hunter was puzzling. He didn't really believe the man had anything to do with the killings, but Rachel's suspicions were compelling. And really, how well did he know Hunter? Actually know him, that is.

It was almost as if the man had been inflicted on him. One disastrous thing after another. Starting with an old homicide where Hunter had known the victim. Later, an investigation into some questionable deaths that'd never been completely answered. Was that ever something. Then there was the guy's past to consider. High on the suspect list in his wife's murder in LA. Fortunately for him, that had worked out. But violence followed Hunter around like an old dog. And don't forget Powers' mentioning the possibility of PTSD. Could there be something to that? After all, he was a combat veteran.

Ah, yes, Powers. How long would she be away at the VA hospital? He knew about her injuries. Halderman had recently filled him in on her military record. Impressive. She hadn't been a behind-the-lines brass hat as he'd once thought. Besides the medals, she'd also received several commendations. Including one for undercover work in breaking up a German drug ring. She was tenacious and tough. He liked working with her.

The cat stared at something invisible in the tree next to the balcony.

~~~

Jack, having grown bored, had left the wine bar for the long walk back to Ashe Street and home, but when he arrived at the house, an impulsive idea came to mind. He went inside to get the keys to his motor scooter.

Traffic was light all the way out North Roosevelt Boulevard. He stopped at the bridge over Blue Bayou and shut off the motor. The water appeared black and viscous, as if it could tar a roof. He looked across the inlet to the dark line of mangroves. No light or campfire glowed anywhere to suggest that someone might be out there. He was certainly glad that *he* wasn't.

He could only guess at what had drawn him here. Some kind of insane wish to bond with the homeless? See what he'd missed when he was down and out? He had to admit the ficus bush he'd slept under then was a far sight better than bedding down in the mangroves. No, he couldn't say why he'd come tonight.

He put on his helmet and was about to start the motor and leave when he saw someone approaching. As the person neared, he could see that it was probably another homeless wearing a filthy fatigue jacket, a watch cap, and worn-out shoes. The man kept his head down and averted his eyes as he passed. Jack felt a twinge of pity for him as he looked after him.

The motor scooter fired up and Jack was quickly on his way back to Ashe Street. Five minutes later the 'homeless' man reached the lot where he'd parked his car and drove to his house.

Chapter 21

Jack missed pasta day at the soup kitchen. Billy had called him that morning with a problem. The boat captain that he'd hired to supply Stella by Starlight with fresh fish had been arrested for transporting illegal aliens. The Coast Guard had gotten a tip and had seized his boat when it re-entered US waters with four Cuban refugees aboard.

"Isn't there someone else?" Jack asked. "Big ocean out there. Lots of fishing going on."

Jack had ridden straight to the Inedible Cafe. Derrick Bean was already there. They sat at a table in the kitchen.

"Can't choose just anybody for the job, Jack," Billy said. "Need somebody working only for you or else you'll be buying picked-over fish. Low-tide stuff's the only thing you get then. Some other fellow's got the fresh catch."

"I asked you to let me buy the fish, remember?" Derrick pointed out in his clipped accent. "Depending on a single source is never a good idea. Especially if you don't know him. Seems like your man had other fish in mind."

Billy snorted in distain.

"Know everybody that's anybody on this damn island," he huffed. "Fisherman don't leave the dock that I don't know him. Been here a hell of a lot longer than you, Derrick."

"More important thing is to know how to tell if a fish is fresh," Derrick smiled. "Starts with the nose."

"Restaurant's not buying fish noses," Billy chuckled. "Want the whole fish. Then maybe you're an expert, hee, hee. Fish noses a specialty down in the islands?"

"I'm talking about the one on your face," Derrick said.

"Hey, want to know how to keep fish from smelling?"

Jack laughed. "Cut off their noses!"

Billy got up from the table.

"Gonna make a pot of coffee. Hope that'll be okay with your nose, Derrick."

Jack gave Derrick a look and both of them stifled a laugh.

"All right, you win," Billy said, returning and refilling their cups. "Don't need for everybody to get in an uproar. Man said he had a secret place way past the reef where he fished. Filled up his boat every day. How the hell was I to know he meant Cuba and he was filling it up with people?"

"Ay, caramba!" Jack hooted.

"Go ahead and laugh," Billy said, grinning himself. "Joke's on me, I guess. But what about tonight?"

"I'll take care it, Billy," Derrick said. "Fellow I know back home is tight with a couple of captains here on Stock Island. He'll put in a word. May have to adjust the menu for tonight, that's all."

The crisis over, Jack said goodbye and went outside. He thought he might still have time to help out at the soup kitchen. He phoned Sonja Lidman before starting his scooter but the call went to her voice mail. He left a message saying that he was available. No sooner than he'd ended the call, his cell phone rang.

"Hi, Sonja," he said. "That was fast."

"Jack?" a strange but familiar voice answered. "Is this Jack Hunter?'

"Uh, yes, may I ask who this is?"

"It's Ruby. Ruby Steele. Remember me?"

~~~

Jewel Banks popped open a can of beer and handed it to Jack.

"Thanks," he said. "And here's to you, Ruby."

He raised the beer in a toast. The three of them sat on the deck of Jewel's boat.

"So what do you think of our girl returning to the fold?" Jewel asked, taking a sip from her own beer.

"I think it's wonderful but what about you, Ruby?"

Ruby sighed.

"You can only stay away from this place for so long before it draws you back."

"I knew for sure she was coming when you were last here," Jewel said to Jack. "Didn't want to spoil the fun."

Ruby smiled at Jewel.

"We already had it set up," Jewel said. "She's staying with me until she gets settled."

"How about the church?" Jack asked. "Going back to it?"

"That's over," Ruby said. "Most of the congregation moved away. The building was sold. Yes, The Church of a Joyful Noise has sailed on."

"Tell him about your band, Ruby," Jewel urged.

"Oh, that. Well, it might be over, too. Couple of us formed a little band in Virginia Beach, that's where I was living. I first stayed with my grandmother in Tampa, then moved to Virginia where my aunt and her husband live. Anyway, we called ourselves the Hot Jupiters."

"I love the name," Jack said.

"Yeah, it was fun. Mainly rock."

"Ruby might play with us," Jewel put in.

"Flamin' Flamingos and Hot Jupiters," Jack whistled. "Better call the fire department."

"It's possible," Ruby smiled.

"Tell you what," Jack said. "Soon as you get your act together, give me a call. I'll headline you at the Undrinkable Bar."

"Where?" Ruby asked with a puzzled expression.

"That's at the Inedible Cafe," Jewel told her. "Our friend here has been busy since you left town."

"Of course he would be," Ruby said. "One other thing,

Jack. You know Ruth and Bobby are living in Swan Quarter. It's not all that far from Virginia Beach. Anyway, we kept in touch."

"How are they?" Jack asked. "I haven't heard from them in I don't how long. I rent her house on Ashe Street. Don't think Ruth knows that it's me. You'll have to come by."

"She knows."

"What? I asked the rental agent not to tell her. Damn!"

"You can't keep a secret from Ruth. She knows everything. But that's not what I was about to say. Ruth and Bobby are on their way to Key West."

Jack felt lost for words.

"I can't believe it," he finally said. "It's like everyone's riding a train on different tracks to the same station."

"They're coming by boat. Trains don't run down here anymore, in case you haven't noticed."

"Oh, I can just see those two on a cruise ship," Jack chuckled, ignoring her sarcasm.

"Not a cruise ship, Jack. It's the boat Bobby's dad used to own. He decided to give up crab fishing. Bobby fixed the thing up and now he and Ruth are going to cruise the islands with it."

Jack shook his head at this. He could just imagine the boat. He only hoped the thing didn't sink before it got here.

"Unbelievable," he said. "Well, that's terrific and good for them. I suppose they'll want to stay in the house."

Then he remembered Derrick.

"Jesus, there's a guy living in the little room out back. He's Billy's cousin. I'll have to find a place for both of us."

"Not to worry, Jack," Ruby smiled. "I imagine they'll stay on the boat at the marina."

""I don't know what to say."

"Try 'welcome' when she knocks on your door."

~~~

It hadn't been a successful night. He was ready to collect

the *T* in his game and it never showed up. What the hell had gone wrong? He'd baited the trap, as it were. Played it ever so cool, as always. Just a mention that he was in the market for some goods, nothing more.

All it got him was wet feet from waiting in the damn mangroves. Maybe that was the problem—he hadn't checked the tide. Fucking place half-flooded. Nobody in his right mind would've been there. Not that these idiots have a mind. They've already fried any brains they might've once had with drugs.

So there'd been nothing left for him to do but leave. Then, on top of that, he'd had the rotten luck to run into some asshole on a motor scooter. Not that he felt he was recognized. Certainly not from that stupid police drawing.

But talk about not being in your right mind, why would anyone come there in the middle of the night to stare at the water? And continuing on the subject of minds, he'd had half a mind to brain him just for the hell of it. He'd gripped the window sash weight in his coat pocket as he'd walked past. Just in case the other half of his mind had decided to go along with it.

Well, another night then. He'd be sure to read the tide charts next time. He plopped a serving of pasta onto the plate.

Chapter 22

"**D**etective Lugo Croaker. How may I help you?"

If she closed her eyes, she would be back in another time. The voice would've taken her there. Silky, confident, cocky just enough to be charming. All that in so few words. The perfect camouflage for a genuine rogue.

"Hello, Detective Croaker. This is Detective Laura Dalton at Van Nuys. I wonder if you have a minute."

"Dalton, you say? I don't believe I know you."

You lying bastard, she thought. Then on the other hand, you probably don't remember, which is even worse.

"I'm not surprised, detective. There must be hundreds of us in the department now."

"Well, ma'am, what can I help you with today?"

"It concerns a case you're working. A jumper named Benny Spring. I understand you're treating it as a suspicious death, that so?"

She had chosen to call it *suspicious* rather than *unclassified,* which left the manner of death open.

"We haven't made a decision," Croaker replied coolly. "Who told you that?"

"Oh, then it's still being looked at as a suicide?"

Croaker took in a breath.

"Why are you asking about Spring, ma'am. If you have any information, I suggest you turn it over to us."

Dalton now noticed the condescension. She wasn't surprised. Croaker had had an attitude toward women even back then. He didn't believe they belonged in police work.

"I think I might indeed have something, Detective Croaker. When would be a good time for us to meet?"

~~~

Leonard Hall had to change buses in San Antonio, Texas. There was a four-hour wait until the next one. He put his small travel bag in a locker and left the terminal to stroll around the area. Near the exit, he spotted an ATM. He tried his luck once more and came away with $400. God, it was so easy. People were truly stupid. He had no sympathy for any of them. They got what they deserved.

He read a poster advertising the San Antonio River Walk. The famous attraction came into being after a disastrous flood washed away fifty people or so. A paved sewer was planned to help control the wild river but smarter thinking shut down that idea. A bypass channel was suggested and today it wound and looped through the city in a two- mile walkway lining its banks. A prosperous walkway for merchants.

It wasn't far from the bus station. Sounded like as good a place as any to pass the time.

Leonard strolled along the river keeping out of the shops and to his thoughts. Foremost, whether to continue on to Key West or perhaps just hang it up here. In Texas? Why not? He had a little seed money, thanks to Benny Spring's largesse. He could start writing again. Maybe Westerns this time. They were making a comeback. Find an independent film company. Show Hollywood what they missed. It was an interesting thought.

Then his insanity, always the winning side, took the floor.

It simply reminded him that he had a score to settle in Key West. He turned back toward the bus station.

~~~

Rachel Powers had spent all day at the VA hospital in Miami waiting for her doctor. No other physician could see her. The snippy nurse told her that she would have to make an appointment for the next morning. That was the system, the woman had said. She made the appointment and then went to her car.

Maybe you can't buck the system, she thought passing through Key Largo westbound on US 1, but you sure can fuck with it.

~~~

Gleason had busied himself most of the afternoon looking up cyanide distributors on the net. That would've been Powers' job had she been around. He hoped to find a lead in the Janice Irwin homicide.

He was surprised at the number of places you could buy deadly chemicals. The companies checked out their customers fairly well. But he figured it was doable to lay your hands on something that could kill a person.

Next, he'd called each distributor, starting with the largest and working his way down. After identifying himself and what he wanted, he was told that he'd need a court order. That they couldn't give out that information.

He'd halfway expected that. Well, getting a warrant could be a problem. He would have to make a good case to the court for wanting one and at this point he was just on a fishing expedition. That wouldn't be good enough.

He was able to ascertain that all of their customers were legitimate businesses—agriculture and industrial. It was explained to him that cyanide is necessary in the manufacturing of paper, textiles and plastics. The salts are used in electroplating and metal cleaning. Cyanide gas is the preferred treatment for pest control.

Then there was also the consideration of how the stuff was shipped. Mostly in large steel drums, sealed tightly. Much more than you needed to make a simple sandwich. Also, you couldn't just order a drum or two with a credit card and a post office box.

Becoming more well-versed in the uses of cyanide at each step of the way, he plodded on. Finally, a small chemical supplier near the bottom of his list located in Ohio sounded promising. The man there said they didn't do all that much business in cyanide anymore due to the economy but occasionally they would get an order for a small amount of potassium cyanide—KCN was its chemical compound, he'd enlightened him—from private research laboratories. However, he would need a warrant before he could give him their names.

Chapter 23

Dalton had made an appointment to meet with Croaker at the Hollywood Community Police Station on N. Wilcox. She'd taken the 101 Freeway to the exit offramp, crawling in traffic the entire way. The Boxster's top was down and the air conditioning on full blast. It was the LA way to drive.

The desk officer sent her back to detectives where the secretary there announced her to Croaker.

"Detective Dalton," he grinned, walking up and giving her the once-over. "Let's go to my desk."

Croaker was a man in his late thirties with just a touch of grey in his hair. He presented himself as someone who worked out regularly. A casting director would definitely have paid him a second look. He wore a very nice dark blue suit, white shirt and red tie. Dalton surreptitiously eyed her own outfit. Tan pantsuit so last year. Fashion wasn't topmost of mind, however. Right now, she'd like to kick him in the balls.

The detective's room was busy with telephone calls coming in, though it was only midmorning. No different from Van Nuys, Dalton thought to herself. The homicide table was at the far end of the room.

"Please have a seat, detective," Croaker gestured.

"Got the place all to yourself today?" Dalton said, aware that no one else was at the table.

"Temporary situation. My d-one is out chasing down a witness. The other two detectives are working an assault that'll probably be upgraded to a homicide. Vic's not doing well at the hospital. *We* stay busy in Hollywood."

Dalton smiled, ignoring the little jab. The fucker even looked the same with those dreamy eyes.

"Well, I won't take too much of your valuable time," she said. "What I'm here about is the Benny Spring case. I understand you're treating it as a suspicious death?"

"Every death is suspicious until determined otherwise," Croaker said, eying her once again.

"Yes, and that's precisely why I'm here. How do you feel about hunches, Detective Croaker?"

"I've followed a few," he said. "Some to somewhere, most to nowhere."

"Good because I have one for you."

She laid out the entire Pamela Ridenour murder investigation, ending with Leonard Hall's arrest and subsequent conviction.

"I didn't realize the full extent of his insanity until the trial," she said. "He promised...how did he put it when they led him out of the courtroom....oh, yeah...I'll be back!'"

She gave a harsh little laugh.

"He actually said that. I mean it was right out of the movies but I believe he meant it. He's a dangerous person."

"Does this have a point, detective?" he asked.

She fixed him with a penetrating look.

Croaker shifted uncomfortably in his chair.

"The point is that knowing Leonard's personality and witnessing his behavior, I believe there may be a possibility that he could be involved in your case."

"Well, be my guest, ma'am. Proceed."

"Leonard Hall was released from prison just days before Benny Spring allegedly jumped from his window. As I said, Officer Francine Mason worked for him while she was a reserve at West LA. According to her, Benny wasn't the kind of person who'd take his own life."

"Happens to the best of people," Croaker sniffed. "You'd be surprised."

"Yes, I know that but somehow it doesn't seem right with Benny. I agree with Officer Mason."

Croaker crossed his arms.

"Let's take a look at Benny Spring," he said. "Here's a successful agent. Got a big office in Century City. A-list clients. Eats at the best restaurants. But then he takes on some no-name writer who's written a for-shit movie script. In Officer Mason's opinion, anyway. We have talked about this case and her phoning you, by the way. So I ask myself why would this guy want to jump out a window. Unless things aren't going all that great. And you know what? They weren't."

This jerk is so full of himself, Dalton thought. Nothing changes.

"What we've been able to determine," he continued, "is Spring wasn't doing well at all. Hadn't been for some time. Wolves knocking at the door. Most of his clients had dropped him. He was forced to move out of the expensive office. Big comedown for a hotshot Hollywood agent, wouldn't you say?"

"So you believe he committed suicide, is that it?"

"In the proverbial nutshell, yes."

"What about the missing items?" Dalton asked. "The money and gun from his desk?"

"Mason was way out of line by telling you that," Croaker said angrily. "Spring's secretary mentioned them but there's no proof that they might've been taken by anyone. Could be he had the gun at his home. As far as money goes, I doubt that there was much, if any, in the desk."

"Was that all, just money and a gun, that was missing?"

"Alleged missing," Croaker said, glaring at her.

"If you insist," she smiled. "How'd you know it was Benny? I mean, right after the incident. Did he have any ID?"

"His secretary apparently came back from lunch, or

129

wherever right after he jumped. She noticed the open door and looked out. Saw the crowd below. Called 911."

"So he didn't have a wallet or anything on him?"

Croaked stifled a yawn.

"The secretary said the guy's wallet wasn't in his coat when she took it off the hanger. And get this. She asked the officer on the scene if he'd take Benny his coat. Thought he might need it. Can you imagine?"

All of this was difficult to imagine, Dalton thought.

"Where was the wallet if it wasn't on Benny?" she asked. "Don't you find that interesting?"

"The guy hit the pavement like you'd dropped a watermelon. Wallet could've sailed to La Cienaga for all I know. Maybe someone found it."

"Back to the gun. Have you checked for it being in his house?"

"We didn't find anything there."

Dalton sat silent for a moment. This guy was incredible!

"Well, it was just a hunch," she smiled. "Some lead somewhere, most go nowhere, right?"

Croaker smiled back.

"Thank you for your interest, Detective Dalton. Anything else I can do for you today?"

"When did you go through academy?" she asked.

"Oh, years ago."

"Me, too. I think I remember you."

A slight tell crossed Croaker's face.

"I'm sorry but I don't think so," he said smoothly. "I know I would remember you."

"Lot of time has passed since then, huh? Oh, there is one more thing I wanted to ask. Were there security cameras in the building?"

She already knew the answer to this because she'd checked with the building manager's office. All the floors had one, including the stairwell.

"Yeah, not much there," he shrugged. "Only thing we got is a guy on the stairs. Building manager said the maintenance man's always going up and down them."

"Could I have a peek? You never know."

"I don't see where there's a need for that, detective," he said, without a trace of friendliness in his voice now.

"Call it professional courtesy."

Croaker sighed and reached to his desk computer. He tapped a couple of keys and the camera footage came up.

Dalton leaned over to better see. The picture showed a person walking quickly down the steps. As he turned on the landing, his face came into view.

"That's Leonard Hall!" Dalton exclaimed excitedly.

~~~

The Greyhound bus motored along Interstate 10 through Louisiana. Leonard looked out the window while passing an off-ramp near Baton Rouge and saw a sign listing the miles to Rachelle Harbor. He wondered what it was like there. Maybe some day. Right now he had other things to do.

~~~

Dalton had spent most of the afternoon at Hollywood. She went straight home from there.

The Valley was unmercifully hot with temperatures nudging the high-nineties. That was in keeping with the hellish time she'd already suffered. She walked in, shed her clothes and headed directly for the shower. Afterwards, she put on a thin robe, poured herself a vodka over ice, and stepped outside onto the small, secluded patio behind her house. The robe slid off her shoulder as she took a seat. She pulled her arm out of the sleeve.

She couldn't get over the day. It'd been so topsy-turvy. And, as she was now just beginning to fully appreciate— totally, completely, devastating.

There'd been Leonard Hall staring into a security

camera. Exactly like before at Pamala Ridenour's condo. On his way to commit a murder then. And now a reversed angle of him leaving another place after—and she was certain of this—yes, after committing yet another murder.

That alone had been almost too much to take in.

But there'd been more. And in this respect, it had been even worse. She had faced Lugo Croaker again. And that had opened a page she'd assigned to the absolute recesses of her mind. It left out not a single detail.

They had both been recruits at the Academy. She was struggling with a certain course. The California Penal Code. In fact, it was giving the entire class a fit. Who would've thought you had to know the law to be a cop? They'd all believed up until then that you only had to say you're under arrest and the court would sort out everything.

Lugo suggested they study together. He had a little apartment in Hollywood which was close by the Academy. She was living in Santa Monica. You could afford to live at the beach back then.

Class ran until nearly seven that evening and she followed Lugo to his place in her boxy little Honda Civic. They'd worked until nearly 10 and both felt they were finally getting somewhere with understanding the damn law. Lugo opened a bottle of wine.

She'd had one glass and said that was enough, that she'd better get home and to bed. It was to be another long day of classes tomorrow. Lugo offered that she stay there. Save her the long drive, why not? She thanked him but declined. He put his arms around her and fondled her breast. She pushed back. Told him to stop.

But he wasn't to be stopped. And he was much stronger.

She missed the next day's class.

Her robe slipped down further and she kicked the thing all the way off. She sat in the nude on her private little patio and cried. The pain that'd been bottled up for so long began to spill out. The cat watched from inside the house.

Chapter 24

"**M**r. Hunter, this is Ruth LaVere."

Jack had gotten up early and was watering the plants around the front of the house when his phone rang.

"Ruth, how are you?"

He was so surprised by the call that he almost dropped the garden hose. Then he remembered that Ruby Steele had mentioned Ruth might be coming to town.

"I'm seasick. And Roy's none the better."

"Where are you?"

"On the Joyful Noise. Bobby says we're now coming up to Boca Chica and will dock at Stock Island."

"That's terrific. I imagine you'll want to come to the house. I'll send a taxi when you're ready."

"No need to bother. We know the way."

Well, this was just something, Jack thought. He hadn't expected them to arrive this soon. Hadn't been sure they were even coming, for that matter. But here they were. Derrick had already left for the restaurant. He'd get in touch with him later. Christ, if they wanted to stay at the house until they were ready to shove off, he'd have to find another place for Derrick.

He rolled up the hose and went inside to get the motor scooter keys.

~~~

Rachel Powers popped a second Aleve before leaving the house. The advertisement promised one pill would get you through the day. She figured another would be good just in case.

During the drive back from the VA Hospital, she'd made up her mind about Jack Hunter. She would call him in for an interview.

The lot was almost full. One slot vacant next to Gleason's. Good, she would run her idea past him.

"On what basis?" Gleason asked, once she'd finished. "Do you have a solid reason for questioning Hunter?"

Hadn't they already been over all of this? she wondered.

"Not questioning, sir. A conversation is all. We know he has been hanging around the homeless shelters. I'm hoping he might have seen something."

"Hanging around the homeless shelters, huh?" he said. "Well, I guess that's cause enough for hauling in his ass."

"Thank you, sir."

~~~

A thick blanket of early morning fog had settled over Interstate 75 north of Ocala, reducing visibility to somewhere near the end of one's nose. But approaching drivers barely gave it a second thought, much less backed off the pedal before speeding into the cloud. Within seconds they plowed into the preceding wave of traffic which had shared the same high-flung attitude and had now become a pileup of wreckage in the middle of the highway. And so it went until by the time the fog lifted, four miles of the Interstate resembled an auto junkyard.

The Greyhound bus carrying Leonard Hall stood along the side of the road at mile three of the twisted and burnt assemblage. Its driver had slowed slightly before becoming completely enveloped by the fog and then had the good fortune to safely pull off the highway. They were saved but wouldn't be going anywhere anytime soon.

News station helicopters chopped overhead. One settled down on an open space near the bus.

~~~

"All I'm saying is you might have to move," Jack said. "Could be they'll stay on their boat. Nothing's been determined."

Derrick shrugged.

"Whatever, Jack, I'll find something. Don't worry."

Derrick was in the kitchen with Jack at Stella by Starlight.

"Thanks, man. I know a couple of guest houses, if you need one. Don't think it'll be for long. So how's everything going here with the new menu and all?"

"Making progress."

Jack waited for a further explanation. All he got was a cool smile.

"Okay. I'll leave you to it."

The guy was probably upset, Jack thought on his way out. He would've been, too. But if Bobby and Ruth wanted to stay in the house, then he'd need the room in back for himself. He got on his scooter and his phone rang. He didn't recognize the caller ID.

"Yeah?" he answered.

"Mr. Hunter? This is Detective Powers with the Key West police department. I wonder if we could talk."

He really didn't need to hear from this woman right now.

"What about?"

"Regarding a homicide."

Gleason's earlier comments flashed through his mind.

"Is this about the homeless killings?"

"That is correct."

"I don't understand why you think I'd have anything of interest."

"You'd be surprised."

"Look I'm kind of busy."

"Mr. Hunter, you said *interest* a moment ago. I think it would be best in yours if you came in for a chat. Today?"

Gleason was right. This was one serious woman. It was time to get her off his back.

"I'll be there within the hour," he said.

Jack rode his scooter home. He'd leave it there and walk. Parking space at the police station was scarce. He changed into a pair of jeans, slipped on a fresh black t-shirt and got out his favorite white linen sports coat that he'd bought years ago in New York and was now beginning to show its age. He stuck the cell phone blanketed with the stainless steel case in the left breast pocket. A similar one had once stopped a slug. He would cut through New Town to N. Roosevelt and the station. It wasn't that far and it was a pleasant day.

Chapter 25

"You're a man of your word," Powers said, looking at her watch. "Said you'd be here within the hour and, my goodness, here you are right on the dot."

The desk officer had notified Powers that Jack was out front. She was walking him back to the interview room. It was the same one she'd used with Tyler Bain. She thought it might be charmed.

"We're in here, sir," she said, opening the door.

Jack went through. A table pushed against the wall and three chairs were the entire furnishings.

"Sit anywhere?" he asked.

"Please, your choice," she gestured.

Jack took a chair at one end of the table. Powers sat opposite.

"First, would you like anything to drink?" she asked. "Coffee, water?"

"I'm good."

"Well, the reason I've asked you to come here is that I'm curious about your connection with the homeless community."

"And why is that, detective? Some law against helping people that I don't know?"

Jack had decided before leaving the house that he wouldn't let this woman intimidate him no matter how serious a person Gleason considered her to be. And where was Gleason, by the way?

Powers smiled.

"Good question, sir," she said. "To answer it, no. Nothing wrong with helping people."

"Then what am I missing?"

"We're investigating several homicides involving the homeless and are looking at anyone who might have information concerning them."

"Are you suggesting I had something to do with them?"

"I didn't say that, sir, let me rephrase. We would appreciate anything you could tell us regarding your association with them."

Jack spread his hands palm up.

"I still don't understand why I'm here," he said. "There must be dozens of people who help out with the homeless. Volunteers, contributors, whatever. Are you calling them in?"

Powers looked at him without expression.

"When I first saw you at KOTS, you told me that you were there looking for help, remember? At first I thought it was some kind of joke you were making. But I gather that you wanted to hire some of their people. True?"

Jack nodded.

"Then, shortly afterwards, I saw you again. You were leaving a transition house this time. The woman in charge said that you were there for the same reason. Offering jobs. That's awfully charitable. You seem to have an affinity for the homeless. Is there some special reason?"

Jack laughed. That goofy lopsided grin of his edged across his face. He unconsciously swiped at it.

"Detective, you've hit the nail on its head," he said, clearing his throat. "I do share something in common with the homeless. An affinity, as you put it. I was once in that position myself. Homeless."

Gleason sat outside the room watching on the monitor. He doubted they'd learn anything helpful, just more than he cared to know about Jack Hunter. He was about to be proved right.

Jack recounted the entire history of his life on the streets. Beginning with his wife's murder and his subsequent flight as a fugitive down to Key West, his eventual redemption and return to Los Angeles, the turn of fortune with a new business enterprise and ending with his vow to help the homeless after surviving a horrendous episode in LA before returning now to Key West.

Gleason had stepped away from the monitor for a cup of coffee and had just returned as Jack wrapped up.

"That's some story," Powers said. "Too amazing not to be true. You can't make that stuff up."

"You can check it for yourself," Jack said. "I don't think I've left anything out."

"Actually, Detective Gleason confirms much of what you've just said."

"Let me ask you something," Jack said. "According to your time line, I arrived here the day you found one of the victims, is that so?"

"That's right, sir. But that in no way means you couldn't have arrived here earlier, does it?"

"Well, a few dozen witnesses back in LA might beg to differ. I can get started with calling them, if you wish. Also, you can phone the airline. I was on Delta."

"I don't think that will be necessary, sir."

All of these *sirs* are getting annoying, Jack thought. Then it occurred to him what it was about her that he'd first sensed. She was ex-military. Not that it was any big deal.

"What were you? Army? Navy?"

For some reason Powers blushed.

"I was Army. Why is that important?"

"Thought so. It's not important. I was also Army."

"I know that. I've seen your military record. Your unit took a lot of casualties. Does that still bother you today?"

Jack looked her in the eye. Hell of a question.

"Sure it does. But if you're thinking I'm some kind of combat mental case going around knocking off your homeless, then lady, you are 'way off the track."

A sharp pain gripped her lower back. She'll triple the Aleve next time.

"You were awarded a Silver Star," she said.

"They pinned a Bronze Star on me in the field. I got a letter after I was discharged saying it had been bumped to the Silver Star. There'd be a ceremony at the local National Guard armory. I didn't attend."

"I also got a Bronze Star. They presented it to me at the hospital. It really doesn't matter, does it?"

Jack drummed his fingers on the table.

"What you did to earn it matters, Lieutenant," he said.

"I think we're finished here, sir. Thank you for coming in."

Chapter 26

"**W**hat's your name, guy?" the man behind the counter said. "Haven't seen you around."

The soup kitchen had been serving lunch since noon. A few stragglers had shown up toward the end but now it was over. This was macaroni and cheese day and they'd run out.

"Wayne," he slurred.

"Gee, Wayne, it looks like you've missed the macaroni. Tell you what, I'll make you a sandwich."

Wayne was a slightly built man in his early twenties with an obvious drug problem. His eyes were watery and the pupils dilated.

The man slapped together a bologna sandwich and handed it to him.

"Where you from, Wayne?"

"Bowling Green."

"What's that near?"

"Glasgow's probably biggest place it's near."

"What? Scotland?"

Wayne did a quiet little laugh.

"No-o-o. It's in Kentucky. That's where I was born."

"What's your last name, Wayne? I know some people in Kentucky."

"Teague."

Something had told him this one was going to be a *T*. He figured him for a pill popper, too. Probably painkillers. He'd seen enough of that with Keith. So he'd pull a switch-up this time. He'd be the seller.

"No shit? There are some Teagues up in Tampa. Any relation?"

"Don't think so," he drawled. "But could be, I guess."

It just got better. Who's going to miss him?

"Staying at KOTS?"

"Soon, soon as I can get in there," he said, stumbling with his words. "They got some crazy rules."

"Tell me about it."

Wayne squinted and wiped at his eyes.

"You need anything?" the man asked.

Wayne looked at him suspiciously. He'd heard this before. Next thing he knows, he's been arrested.

"A little help to get your balance back. People over there at KOTS don't understand that with all those rules they keep making."

Wayne was beginning to hurt something awful and if getting his balance back, whatever the hell that was, would help then he was all for it.

"What're you saying, man?"

"I can do you some OxyContin."

"Kind of short on money right now. Only have a couple of bucks."

"You know where the Blue Bayou is?"

"That the place over by the bridge? Sure, I know it. Where I'm staying 'cause they won't let me in KOTS."

"Go to the bridge tonight around ten. I'll be standing at the bottom of it. Right by the water. Don't worry about the money. Catch you later."

~~~

Jack was sitting on his front porch enjoying a beer after walking home from the police station. He had run through the entire interview several times but still hadn't come to any conclusion. Powers obviously had taken a serious interest in him at some point. But now it appeared be over. Was she flighty? Maybe she was just thorough. He only hoped she was satisfied.

A taxi pulled up at the curb and sat for a moment. Then the rear door opened and an apparition appeared.

"Jack, spare one of those cold ones?" Bobby Sunshine yelled from the cab.

Ruth LaVere clambered out behind him carrying a birdcage containing a parrot. The cab driver retrieved a couple of bags from the trunk and placed them on the sidewalk. He shook his head, and without a word, got back in his car and drove off.

"Old place is looking spiffy, Jack," Bobby said, looking around while mounting the steps, Ruth at his heels with the cage.

Jack stood waiting with a large grin on his face. Everything was right again. For the present, anyway, he added to himself.

"Let me get those bags. You all go on inside."

~~~

"I'm kind of nervous about Leonard Hall being on the street," Francine Mason said. "I mean, if he killed Benny, then what's to keep him from coming after all of us? He's crazy enough."

"Just be cautious," Dalton told her. "He'll soon be picked up. Besides, all anyone knows right now is that he was in Benny's building at the time. Doesn't mean he had anything to do with his death."

Mason had caught Dalton at home before she'd left for Van Nuys. She had taken the morning off and slept in. It'd been a rough night after the previous day with Lugo Croaker.

"Detective Croaker's taking the credit for spotting him," Mason said. "Has the lieutenant and captain involved, too."

"I'm not surprised. He can have it. Question is, what's he doing about bringing him in?"

"Beyond my pay scale," Mason laughed. "I got into trouble with Croaker for talking with you."

"Sorry about that. Croaker said he'd spoken to you. Tell me something, what's the word on him? You called him a

Neanderthal. Does he have a reputation for being a jerk? He certainly impresses me that way."

"More for being a smooth operator. But apparently he has a thing about women. Doesn't believe they belong in police work. I heard there'd been several complaints of sexual harassment. Got a commendation at Southwest. Probably cancelled out the complaints and got him out of there. Now he's a big city detective in Hollywood. He's very political."

"Okay. Take care, Francine. Call me anytime. I've got to go to work."

Dalton hung up and took a sip of cold coffee. Sexual harassment, she thought. She wondered how far that went. A pat on the fanny or more? And with how many women?

After Croaker had raped her, she'd done what most victims did. Gone home and showered. She had felt dirty. Reporting the assault was out of the question. She could have, of course, but it would've been impossible to prove. And it would have sunk any chance of her becoming a police officer. She'd just had to suck it up. Hope he hadn't given her the clap or worse.

Today things might've been different. Society had taken a stronger stance against that kind of predation. People were far less accepting of deviant behavior. Not in every case but the odds of getting a good outcome favored the victim now. Sometimes.

So maybe she'd look into this sexual harassment stuff. There still might be some justice out there. And justice served delayed was just as sweet.

She flicked on the television to catch the last of the morning news. Footage of an unimaginable traffic accident in Florida. On the scene a reporter interviewing some bus passengers that'd been involved. And right in the background, leaning against the bus, stood Leonard Hall.

Chapter 27

Bobby Sunshine's unruly hair had gone completely white to match his shaggy beard. A curious upturned frown-line now creased his forehead. It accompanied his perpetually downcast scowl. He was like one of those old trick drawings of a face that would become another with a different expression when you turned the picture around. Only Bobby's wouldn't have changed no matter which way his was turned.

"You repaint in here?" he asked Jack. "What was wrong with the old color?"

They were in the living room. Ruth was putting away her things in one of the bedrooms. Roy sat quietly on his perch in the cage eyeing both of them.

Roy was an African Grey parrot that belonged to Ruth and possessed a talent for singing.

"Had to do a little work on the outside," Jack said. "Thought I'd just freshen up everything while I was at it."

He was unsure if it would be wise to tell exactly why the work was necessary. That an arsonist had set fire to the house hoping to burn him up along with it.

"You have a roomer out back," Bobby stated. "Guess that provides a little income. That so?"

"That's not the reason he's here, Bobby. He's the new chef at the restaurant and needed somewhere to stay. Just temporary."

"You still working at that place?"

"Have two of them now. Yes, I'm still involved."

Hadn't he told them about he was doing? He was sure he'd written. Must not have.

"Derrick Bean is the fellow staying here," Jack said. "I'll

have to call him, see if he's found a new place."

"Hell, Jack, you can't just ask a tenant to up and move. I know it's a little crowded in here for the time being, but you've got a responsibility to the man. Why, it would be unethical to throw him out. You should know that."

"It's not a problem, Bobby, believe me."

"No, no, can't have the poor man with no place to go. We'll be here for just a short while. No more than a couple weeks or so. The weather's nice now. Set up a cot on the porch for yourself and it'll be just like camping, son."

"Bobby..."

"I'd sleep there myself but the ol' back' been acting up." He placed his hand behind his waist and groaned.

"I'll call Derrick. On second thought, I'll go see him."

Jack left the house on his scooter to ride over to Stella by Starlight. Derrick was in the kitchen.

"Thought you might be my fishmonger," he said. "Suppose to be bringing some hog fish."

"Sounds good," Jack said. "I'll come back tonight."

"Be sure to make a reservation."

"That sounds even better. Business must be up."

Derrick nodded.

"About your having to move," Jack said, "that's no longer necessary."

"Oh, the people aren't coming?"

"They're here. I've decided to take a room somewhere else. The back is still yours."

"No, Jack, that's very kind of you but I don't have any problem with moving. I appreciate what you've already done."

"Nope. It's settled. See you later."

~~~

"Anybody know who heads up homicide at Hollywood?" Dalton asked the robbery table.

She'd just come into the detectives room at Van Nuys.

Her boss, Detective Three Tom Bradshaw, had left for the day. Several detectives were still there at their tables.

"I think it's Bob Moyer," one of them said.

"Yeah, it's Moyer," the other confirmed. "He just made dick three."

She phoned Hollywood and was put through to the head of homicide. After introducing herself, she explained that she had shared information with Detective Croaker on the Benny Spring case and now she'd recently learned something new. She realized she was way out of bounds by going around Croaker.

"This person you saw on television news is the same one Detective Croaker showed you from the building's security camera" Moyer said. "And now he's in Florida. Is that what you're saying?"

"Yes, I'm certain that he's the same person. Detective Hagen and I arrested him for the Ridenour murder a few years back when we were at West LA."

"Think I knew Hagen," Moyer said. "Called him the *trash man* because he went through everything checking a crime scene. He's retired now, right?"

"Raising mules on a ranch in Arroyo Grande. He'll make you a deal on one if you're interested."

"Might be hard to keep a mule in my condo. But back to this news program, have you spoken to Detective Croaker about it?"

"No, frankly I was very disturbed when I saw that Leonard Hall was in Florida and I believe I know why he's there."

Dalton told him about Leonard's behavior at the trial, the obvious animosity he'd shown toward Jack and the threats he had made against everyone. She also mentioned the missing gun and billfold from Benny Spring's office.

"You know we have no evidence of foul play in Mr. Spring's death." Moyer said. "It's a probable suicide. Is

Detective Croaker aware of this television news story?"

"I don't know, sir. I haven't spoken with him."

"Yet you've called me. I find that odd, detective."

"As I said, I was upset when I saw Leonard Hall standing by that bus and maybe I've overstepped bounds by going straight to you. I apologize for that and in no way doubt Detective Croaker's capability, but I believe Hall is on his way to Key West to harm Jack Hunter. I thought your rank and experience might allow you to make an informed decision about what to do. I realize this all sounds pretty crazy but so is Hall. He certainly had motive with Benny Spring. He believes the man screwed him over. He has no problem with violent death. I think that possibility needs to be taken seriously."

"Let me get this clear," Moyer said slowly. "Leonard Hall, fresh out of prison, is on a revenge bender. Has already murdered one person and is now heading for Florida to do more of the same. That is what you think?"

Dalton paused before answering.

"It's not only what I think, Detective Moyer, I truly believe he's capable of causing harm. I have a copy of a routine psychological exam given while he was in prison. He apparently passed the sociopath's test with flying colors. He's one-hundred percent. At his trial, he showed absolutely no remorse or accepted any responsibility."

"Excuse me, Detective Dalton, let me interrupt here," Moyer cut in. "First of all, Detective Croaker is the lead in this investigation and this is Hollywood's case. Are we clear on that? Wait, wait. I'll repeat it. This is Croaker's case. Now, do you understand?"

"Yes, sir."

"You're on thin ice here, detective, but I'm going to cut you some slack. I'll be out of town for a couple of days, so if you have any more theories to share concerning this investigation, do it with Detective Croaker. As I said, it's his case."

~~~

"How long will you need the room?"

"Maybe two weeks," Jack said. "Might be longer."

"You've stayed with us before?"

"Yeah, it was a year or so ago. Don't remember exactly."

"Well, then you qualify for a ten percent return guest discount," the clerk beamed.

Jack had once spent a single sleepless night at the Straits Motel on South Street after being attacked by a mugger. He'd needed a place off the main drag then for safety's sake. Now it was to keep his sanity.

The clerk handed him the room keys.

It could've been the same cramped little space he'd had before. TV set looked newer, he thought. Flat screen instead of the old RCA box. Someone in the room next door flushed the toilet. The water pipes in his bathroom began to sing in harmony.

~~~

To his surprise, Jay Halderman felt relieved when the news came down. Another officer had been named to replace the captain. He'd been bucking for the job and thought he had made the cut. But a lieutenant from another department had aced him out.

So now the suspense was over and he could get back to doing the work he was best at. Running homicide. He called Gleason to come into his office.

"What's up, Lieutenant?"

"Have a seat, Earl. Suppose you know I was angling for the captaincy after Mahoney left. Had put in my papers and all. Well, that position's gone to another officer."

Gleason had felt something along those lines was in the air. He'd known Captain Mahoney had been offered the chief's job in Key Largo. It explained the LT's behavior the past few weeks.

149

"Well, I'm both sad and glad for you, Jay."

"Thank you, Earl. Now, let's get back to business. Where are we with these homeless killings?"

"Still no real prospects. Powers interviewed Jack Hunter—dropped him from the suspect list. Not that there ever was a list."

"Damn, but you never thought he had anything to do with it anyway, did you?"

"No, but she wasn't so sure. I let her run with it."

"Where do you go next?"

"Both Powers and I do believe the murderer is connected with the homeless program. Whether it's someone working in it or a member of the community. I think we should go under cover—put a couple of officers on the street."

"All right, you're in charge of the operation, Earl. But watch the budget."

~~~

Jack had returned home and was killing time before leaving. He and Bobby were on the front porch watching the day end. Ruth called from inside.

"Bedtime for Roy," she said. "Jack, why don't you read him a story?"

Roy loved to be read stories from the Bible. That had been one of the conditions Ruth had laid down for Jack when he'd first inquired about a room at her house several years earlier. Reading to Roy was considered part of the rent. Didn't matter that for all purposes Jack was no longer that room renter. It didn't matter to Ruth. She was here and Roy was due a bedtime story.

Jack and Bobby went into the living room where they waited.

"Well, my good feathered friend," he greeted, reaching into the birdcage, "how about a few passages from the Book of Ruth?"

The parrot perched on his arm and Jack took him to a chair and sat down. He'd no sooner opened the Bible when someone knocked on the screen door.

"Hello everyone. I'm Derrick Bean."

"Come in, come in, son," Bobby shouted, and then in an aside to Ruth, "That's Jack's tenant. He's a big one, ain't he?"

"Hope everyone likes fish," Derrick said, a large cardboard box in hand.

Bobby sniffed the air.

"Something sure smells good."

"Hogfish," Derrick said, opening the box top.

Jack stood up and looked inside where a huge broiled fish lay on a platter surrounded by cooked vegetables.

"I think you'll find the braised veggies accompany the fish very well," Derrick said in his best London accent.

Jack was more impressed by the size of the hogfish.

"How much did that thing weigh, Derrick?" he whispered. "Must be a hundred-dollar fish! And you brought it here for them to eat?"

"Shhh, Jack, it was the last one."

"There's a refrigerator at the restaurant, Derrick."

"Fresh fish every day like Billy says."

Ruth put Roy back in the cage without his story and they all went into the kitchen where Derrick set the table. Jack had to admit when they'd finished dinner that Billy was right, the man did indeed know how a fish ought to be done.

"Wow, look at the time," Jack said. "I'd better be going."

He hated the thought of riding the scooter to the lousy motel. What he would like to do is collapse in his own bed.

"Yep, after eleven," Bobby yawned.

They all got up from the dinner table.

"Don't worry about the dishes, Ruth," Derrick said. "I'll wash up."

Jack shot him a look. Derrick grinned back.

~~~

Beneath the bridge at Blue Bayou, Wayne Teague rested on the inlet's bottom staring with unseeing eyes up through the murky water.

Chapter 28

"You'll be helping Mike today," Sonja Lipman said. "We're doing some deep cleaning so we won't be serving lunch. Should've hired a professional service for this kind of job but our budget can't afford it."

Jack followed her to the kitchen. A man was scrubbing the walls. He had on a pair of overalls and wore a bandana around his neck.

"Hi, Mike," she said brightly. "Brought you some relief."

"I'm Jack Hunter. I believe we've met before."

"Might've been before my new hairdo," Mike laughed, placing his hand on his shaved head. "Got rid of the grey."

"Where do I start?"

"The stove's next," Mike motioned. "Have to take it apart. Do the burners first. It's kind of a dirty job. Too bad you don't have some work clothes."

Sonja left the two men.

"Have you been with the kitchen long?" Jack asked, making chitchat.

"Yeah, guess I have."

Jack quickly had the burners removed. He laid them on the floor.

"I believe you said that you were a lawyer," he said.

"You've got a good memory, Jack. Spray some of that oven cleaner on the burners and around inside where they came out. Actually, I've been connected one way or another with both the homeless and recovery programs for more years than I care to admit."

"Was your social work related to your law business?"

"It was related to a relation, Jack. My little brother. Poor guy was in and out of rehab and shelters all his life.

You ever use drugs?"

"No, never saw that much in them."

"You're a smart man. Keith, that was my brother, couldn't keep away from them."

"Is he clean now?"

"In a way. He died from an overdose."

"Jesus, that's terrible. I'm really sorry, Mike."

Mike pulled out a pack of cigarettes.

"Let's take a break," he said, shaking out one and offering it to Jack.

"Thanks but I've quit smoking for the time being."

"Keith was a surprise baby," Mike said, lighting up. "I was sixteen when he was born. Our parents split soon afterwards. Mom was an alcoholic and my dad just walked out. Grandparents took us in. Anyway, I finished college, went to law school, got married and sort of inherited my brother. The old folks could barely care for themselves by then, much less Keith. He came to live with us."

"How'd that work out?"

"My wife eventually divorced me."

"That sounds cold."

"Keith was one of those people who was always trying to get it together but never could make it stick. The few times he'd come close, he'd go right off the track again. Drugs. Rehabs. One after the other. He'd disappear and I'd find out later he'd been living on the street. He became my life's work. That's why my wife left—I had no time for her. It was all Keith all the time. Afterwards, I moved us both down here. You know, thinking a change of scene might help. Worked for awhile, too. Now, he's gone for good."

Jack felt embarrassed. Not that he wasn't sympathetic but this all seemed so private. The guy must need someone to unload on.

"I'm glad you don't use drugs, Jack. Personally, I think every goddamn drug dealer should be hung out to dry. Some countries execute them. What's your opinion on that?"

The conversation was now becoming uncomfortable.

"How're the burners looking? Clean enough?" Jack said.

~~~

A tourist had spotted the body. The woman was walking across the bridge and stopped to take a picture. She looked down at the water and straight into a deadman's eyes.

"He's caught up on something," Gleason said.

He and Powers had just arrived on the scene. The area had been taped off and one lane of traffic closed. They stood on the bridge above where the body lay.

"The current isn't moving him. We'll need a police diver."

"Water doesn't look all that deep," Powers said. "Do you think he jumped?"

"Could've been an accident. People do nutty things. Let's go down there."

The two detectives followed a narrow path leading through the brush to the water's edge.

"I can't make him out from here," Powers said. "Too much reflection."

"Looks like it's about five feet deep," Gleason estimated. "Tide's about finished coming in. Probably rise only a few more inches, if that."

"Kind of shallow for a swan dive off the rail, sir."

"See what he looks like when we get him out. Maybe he hit bottom and broke his neck."

Powers noticed the ground was disturbed near where she stood.

"Wonder if people camp here, too?" she said, poking around. "I know it's not quite in the Bayou.

"Look, there's some money," Gleason said, reaching into a small shrub. "Six bucks wadded up. Not much to kill somebody for."

"The ground cover's pretty torn up, sir," Powers said. "Could've been a scuffle. Argument or a robbery."

"Be careful where you step, Rachel. Whatever happened to our swimmer might've started here. Let's not miss anything."

The police divers arrived in a rigid-hull inflatable boat. This was the procedure anytime a drowning victim had to be removed, even from a shallow inlet such as this one. To wade in from land and drag the body onto the bank could contaminate evidence.

It took them about five minutes to set up their equipment and then one of them rolled off the side into the water.

"Your victim's snagged on a mangrove shoot, Detective," the diver called to Gleason after surfacing. "I don't see anything else around the body. I'll cut him loose."

"Okay, officer, I'm considering this entire area to be a possible crime scene."

"We'll take the vic back to the dock. I'll call Sheriffs to meet us."

Monroe County Sheriff's Department was involved in any death, although this would be Key West's investigation.

Gleason and Powers watched as Wayne Teague's body was hauled on board.

"We'll meet them at the dock," Gleason said.

A glint of something bright at the water's edge caught Power's eye. She reached down for it.

"Buried treasure, sir," she said, handing a small gold charm to Gleason.

"Something's written on it. I can't make out what it says. Maybe you've got better eyes, Rachel."

Powers took back the charm.

"*Thank you*," she read. "*Keith.*"

Chapter 29

Dalton had gotten the telecast of the Florida highway pileup off the television station's website. She was showing it to Croaker at Hollywood.

"That's him," she said. "What do you think, detective?"

"I'm not sure. Picture's small. Kind of grainy, too."

"I know what Hall looks like, Detective Croaker. And I'm telling you, that's him on the TV screen."

"Like I said, the picture's grainy."

Dalton gritted her teeth.

"Yeah, it's too grainy," Croaker said. "But even if it *was* clear, I'd not be sure he's the same person on the security camera. He was in LA. This one, whoever you think he is, is in Florida. Other side of the country. Could be anybody. Just a lookalike."

"You're wrong," Dalton said firmly. "He's Leonard Hall. Did you read the other stuff I sent? About the guy being a nut?"

Croaker rolled his eyes.

"What about the bus?" Dalton snapped. "Shouldn't you get a passenger list?"

Croaker choked a laugh.

"What? You think Hall would've used his real name to buy a ticket? Waste of time, lady."

"Careful who you call a lady, detective."

Dalton left Croaker at the station. One thing she had learned. Croaker was a lousy cop and probably wouldn't follow up on Hall. She was just getting into her car to drive back to Van Nuys when she had a thought. It was a long shot and she really didn't know if it would be worth anything. She called Jack Hunter's old ad agency and asked for

William Wardell.

"Detective Dalton, he said. "Don't tell me you've found my car."

"I didn't know it was missing."

"Some jerk stole it from the parking garage. Brand-new Lexus. Hate to admit it, but I have to take some of the blame. I keep a spare key under the fender. One of those little boxes with a magnet on it."

"Bad idea. But finding your car is a job for Santa Monica police. The reason I'm calling is to ask if you or or anyone at your business has had any contact with Leonard Hall. He was recently released from prison."

"Jesus Christ! Little early for parole, wasn't it? No, he certainly hasn't called me. I wouldn't think he'd be in touch with any of our people."

Dalton didn't want to alarm him further by mentioning her suspicions. And actually, there was no real reason why Leonard would want to speak with any of them. Other than her hunch he might be out for revenge.

"Leonard Hall is a dangerous person," she said. "And should he try to get in touch with you or anyone at your business, call the police."

"Hey, you don't think he's the one who took my Lexus, do you?"

~~~

Wayne Teague lay stretched out on the wooden planks of the dock. He'd been carefully lifted from the police boat and placed there. Gleason squatted beside him.

"Those marks on his neck," he noted to Powers. "Could be from strangulation."

"There're bruises on his face," Powers said. "Looks like his nose is broken, too. Fight?"

"I don't think he got any of this is from diving off the bridge. Although I guess he could've plowed into the bottom if he'd jumped headfirst."

"Wonder if that charm belonged to him?" Powers said. "If it did, then he wouldn't have lost it by diving."

"No, he wouldn't have," Gleason said. "Stronger chance of it coming off in a fight."

"A couple of his fingernails are broken. Maybe whoever attacked him has something to show for it."

"Yeah, we'll make a note of that. Poor guy doesn't look all that healthy. I mean, other than his being dead. We'll get a photo and check with the shelters. I couldn't find any identification on him."

"So what do you think, sir? Did he drown or was he choked?"

"That's what the medical examiner will tell us."

Wayne was placed on a gurney and rolled to the waiting van for his ride to the morgue. Gleason and Powers drove back to the bridge.

"Christ, it's hot down here," Gleason complained.

"It's not a very good camp site," Powers said.

They had walked off most of the area around the base of the bridge.

"I don't believe anyone was camping," Gleason said. "Our victim and killer were here for another reason. There are no signs of this being a permanent site. Think we've probably found all we're going to. Let's climb back up to the street."

"Maybe it was another drug deal," Powers said. "Could've turned into a robbery and gone on to homicide"

"Nothing new there. Hold on, what's this?"

Gleason noticed a couple of dark red smears on the concrete footing of the bridge. He bent down for a closer look.

"Have the techs check this out for blood," he told Powers.

~~~

Dalton's phone chirped. It was William Wardel. She

was reluctant to take the call. Her own work was piling up. She'd already spent too much time on a case that belonged to Hollywood. She certainly didn't need to stick her nose in another one that was Santa Monica's. But she had asked him to let her know if he heard anything from Leonard Hall. This could be it. She picked up.

"Just got a phone call from Santa Monica police," he said excitedly. "Cops in Phoenix have my Lexus. Can you believe that?"

"Phoenix?"

"Couple of kids had it. Rolled through a stop sign. Cops checked the plates and saw it'd been stolen."

This was interesting, Dalton thought.

"You're saying two children took your car from the garage in Santa Monica and drove it all the way to Arizona?"

"Apparently. I don't know the details but the car is there. I'm flying out tomorrow to pick it up."

"Glad your car was recovered," she said. "Get rid of that spare key box."

She ended the call. None of this made sense. That expensive Lexus would've gotten a one-way trip to Tijuana, not been taken on a joy ride to Arizona. She phoned Santa Monica police and learned that the Phoenix department had said the suspects were two local youths who told them they'd found the car parked on the street with the keys in the ignition. One of them had been arrested before. The Phoenix cops speculated that the car was probably being delivered to a Mexican car theft ring.

She asked Santa Monica if the Arizona forensics team had pulled any prints from the car. No need for prints, they said—already had the bad guys. She knew that but she'd had another wild card in mind.

Who'd driven Wardel's spanking new Lexus to Arizona? And who would've known about the spare set of keys? Maybe his prints were on the car. And just for the fun of it, how about Leonard Hall being that person? He was familiar with the agency's parking and might've known about Wardel's habit of hiding the spare key. Warden had ID'd him in the photo lineup, so in Leonard's mind he deserved some form of punishment. He could have considered stealing the car would be sufficient. Fortunately for Wardel, a much less violent reprisal than Benny Spring had suffered. But why then did he drive to Phoenix and dump the car?

She admitted all of this was blue-sky thinking almost to the point of being absurd. But nothing about this case made sense. Leonard Hall released on a technicality. Benny Spring jumping out of a window. Wardel's car turning up in Phoenix. Hall seen in Florida. She needed hard evidence to back up her suspicions.

Then something clicked. She called back Wardel. She'd have to somehow deal with the extra time.

~~~

Detective Lugo Croaker had just gotten off the phone with Benny Spring's secretary. She had just been going over the charges on Benny's credit card statement while preparing to close the account. She had found an ATM withdrawal that she couldn't account for. Should she keep the account open to see if others came in, she wanted to know? Croaker told her that it was probably just a mistake by the credit company, that they were famous for being behind with their postings, but if any more charges showed up to let him know.

Chapter 30

"**I** can tell you right now this man didn't drown," the medical examiner stated. "He was dead before he went into the water."

Dr. Blake Hardy had been at the Lower Keys Medical Center when Wayne Teague's body was brought in. Normally, he would've had to drive down from his office in Marathon. Powers and Gleason were with him in the morgue.

"See these finger marks on his throat?" Hardy asked. "And this larger one? That would be from the thumb. So I suspect manual strangulation. Throttling. Of course, the full autopsy will either confirm that or not. But I do believe we'll discover thorax damage and a fractured hypoid bone once we get inside. One thing we won't find is water in his lungs. I'll put money on that."

Powers glanced at Gleason.

"Wonder if the bloody smear was his or belonged to whoever killed him?" she asked.

Hardy looked up.

"We discovered a trace of what might be blood at the scene," she told him. "Forensics have it."

"They can tell you if it's human or not and if so, the type," Hardy said. "This victim was pretty badly beaten before he died. I'd say somebody had it in for him. Good chance your blood smear belongs to him."

"Think we can get an autopsy report soon?" Gleason asked.

"Soon as I've completed the autopsy, detective."

~~~

He removed the neckerchief and examined the wound

at the base of his neck in the bathroom mirror. It'd been a nasty little gash. He carefully pulled off the dressing and cleaned the area around the wound with hydrogen peroxide. It felt somewhat better.

He'd misjudged. The kid had been stronger than he looked and knew something about fighting. The little bastard's last effort was to dig in his nails. He should've seen a manicurist before coming out. He laughed at the joke. Funny scene, though. Well, he had gotten the upper hand at the end. Another joke.

Losing that charm was no joke however. He hadn't realized it was missing until he'd come home. Of all the lousy luck, how do you replace something like that? You don't. Once things cool down, he'd go back and look for it.

~~~

Dalton met Wardel at the agency and they took the elevator down to the parking garage.

"If you spot the key box, don't touch it," she said. "I'll put it in an evidence bag."

Wardel nodded.

"It's blue and about three inches long," he said. "The light isn't too great down here. Hope we can find it."

"I brought a flashlight."

"That's my slot up there."

Dalton played the flashlight around the parking space.

"I don't see anything," Wardel said.

"Just keep your eyes open. I'm going to look behind those curbs near the wall."

The beam reflected off a small object lying on the floor two spaces over.

~~~

"Billy, can you talk to him?"

Jack had dropped by the Inedible Cafe on his way to the motel.

"What's there to say, Jack? Restaurant's picked up since

Derrick took over. Making some money for a change, hee-hee."

"Well, that's the point, Billy. Giving away a hundred-dollar fish because it was the last one and he didn't want to keep it in the refrigerator is silly. Don't you agree?"

Billy's attention had switched elsewhere.

"Did you hear what I said?"

"Sorry, Jack, it's not that I didn't hear you, it's just that I had another thought in my head and it wouldn't get out of the way."

"Never mind."

"You see, Jack, Derrick asked me about that fish first. Said he wanted to do something nice for your guests and you since you'd been so good about letting him stay at your place. Not wanting to stick that fish back in the refrigerator had nothing to do with it. Derrick's no fool."

Well, Jack felt like one.

"I don't know what to say, Billy."

"Don't have to say anything. What about that girl band you wanted? Think you can get them for a night?"

"I'll line them up."

Jack left Billy and returned to the Straits Motel. He really did feel badly about his attitude toward Derrick and deserved the admonishing Billy had given him. The guy was turning around Stella by Starlight and if he needed someplace to stay temporarily, well, he was welcome at his house. Also, Bobby and Ruth had to leave eventually. Didn't they?

He took a shower and flopped on the bed to watch some television. The motel featured HBO but he'd seen the movie. He flicked off the set and let his mind wander through the events of the day. They'd done a good job on the kitchen. He was especially proud of the stove.

Mike was an odd duck, he thought. Seemed to really be into helping out. He'd given up everything for his kid brother. Wife, law practice, home. Quite a sacrifice. But there was a strange vibe about Mike that was disturbing. A true believer. Remarkably, it brought to mind a murderous individual he'd known in Los Angeles. Well, that was a pretty extreme comparison. He definitely didn't think that of Mike. Poor man was on a mission to serve, that was all. Just like he was.

Next door the TV suddenly blasted at full volume. The HBO movie. Rather than make an issue, he got up and dressed.

The sun had set, leaving the sky with a token of light. He walked over to Duval in the afterglow and down to Vinos. Pausing on the sidewalk, he saw the place was empty. Not looking for company but neither seeking solitude, he kept moving.

Lower Duval was shoulder-to-shoulder. He jaywalked mid-block between Eaton and Caroline Streets, cutting between the standing traffic. Had he bothered to look at the occupants of the car he walked behind, he might've recognized Detective Rachel Powers in the driver's seat. He wouldn't have known the two scruffy homeless men with her.

"I'll turn at the next block and let you out," Powers said. "This traffic sucks."

"Should've come the back way," one of the men told her.

"I know. Just wanted to see Duval."

"Still a tourist, huh?"

"Well, you have to admit it is kind of interesting."

"Gets old quick, detective."

Powers hadn't found it easy finding the officers for the job she had in mind. The problem was that most of the cops were in good shape. She needed puny. Showing some road wear. Tattered clothes, uncombed hair and a one-day beard was the best she could do with the only two available.

She'd briefed them at the station. Do the slow walk.

Hang at the peripheral of crowds. They were there mainly to observe. Should anyone get chummy, play along but call her.

"We'll give this a couple of hours," Powers said, as the car in front inched ahead another length. "At last, here's Caroline."

There were so many people, she had to wait almost through the green light before she could make her turn off Duval.

"I'll be just in front of those bikes."

The two cops got out and Powers drove past a line of Harleys and parked.

Jack lingered in front of Sloppy Joe's listening to the band. He noticed two men approaching who, judging from their appearance, were probably living on the street. He remembered the poor soul in the alley that'd asked for spare change and he'd snubbed. He decided that he wouldn't let it pass this time.

"Hey, guys," he said, stopping them. "You want something to eat?"

The two cops exchanged glances.

"Sure," one of them said.

"There's a pizza joint," Jack said, pointing. "I'll buy you dinner."

The three of them crossed Duval, one lagging behind to radio Powers.

"You grab a table while I order," Jack said.

Powers walked in just as Jack was picking up his pizza.

"You continue to fascinate me, Mr. Hunter," she said, taking a seat at the table with the two undercover officers. "Mind if I join you and your friends?"

"Please do," Jack said, surprised at seeing her. "Fellows, this is Detective Rachel Powers. She's with the Key West police department."

The two officers remained silent.

"Have you all known each other long?" she asked Jack.

"Just met," Jack said. "Offered to buy dinner."

"Well, that's awfully generous to do for someone you've just met. You do that often for strangers? Buy them dinner?"

"Nope. First time ever. But now that you mention it, that's a good idea. Maybe I'll keep at it."

"I see. This is part of your new good samaritan role?"

"If you want to call it that, yes."

"My advice to you, Mr. Hunter, is be careful about who you invite to dinner."

Jack leaned back in the chair, a serious expression on his face.

"Look, detective, I saw these two guys and I just figured they might be hungry. Like I told you, I've been there myself."

"That's all well and good," she said, "but you've interrupted a police operation. These two gentlemen are undercover officers with the KWPD. Now, we have to go home."

Chapter 31

Leonard Hall must favor his left hand, Dalton thought, as she read the report from the print technician. She mentally tried opening the thing herself. In her mind, she used her right thumb and finger to slide back the top. The other way seemed awkward. Maybe Leonard was ambidextrous. It didn't really matter. The techs had found a clear left-hand thumb and index fingerprint matching Leonard's on the top and bottom of the small metal key case.

For some crazy reason that only he could've had, Leonard obviously had stolen William Wardel's car and driven to Phoenix where it was then re-stolen by a couple of kids. Next thing you know, Leonard shows up in Florida standing next to a bus. What a wacky chain of events.

She called the Greyhound station in Phoenix and asked to speak with a supervisor.

~~~

"Why Duval?" Gleason wanted to know.

"Because it was there," Powers said.

"C'mon."

He and Powers were at the police station. The two undercover cops had returned to regular duty.

"Nearly all of the homicides have taken place around the Blue Bayou," she said, "but we don't know where the victims first met the suspect. Or for that matter, at this point, if it's the same person or a whole gang. Of course, the selection could be random. But I believe there's a method, a specific reason for choosing these particular victims. And therefore, they had to know their killer. And I do believe it is a single person. So where did they first meet?"

"On Duval Street? That's a hell of a walk from there to the Blue Bayou."

"Maybe Duval was wrong, sir. I don't know. I wanted to try something different."

"Well, you netted Jack Hunter," Gleason laughed. "You still believe he's involved in this?"

"No, not involved in the murders. I can't say exactly what turned the page with me about him. Just doesn't click. But his involvement with the homeless has made me think."

"Go on."

"Mr. Hunter is sincere about wanting to help. He first looked into hiring some people from the shelters. Apparently, that didn't work out. So he volunteers at the soup kitchen."

"I'm not sure I see where this is going, Rachel."

"There are a lot of volunteers in the different homeless organizations. Maybe we should start looking at some of them. Possibly there's a connection. Craziness or something."

Gleason got up from the table and went to get a cup of coffee.

"Didn't we go over this before?" he asked, returning. "You made a list of the volunteers, I believe."

"That's true, sir. But then I began to focus on Mr. Hunter."

Gleason nodded.

"There was nothing wrong with that," he said. "I never really believed Hunter was good for the murders but no harm done in looking at him. So, yes, let's concentrate on the volunteer angle."

"Should we stick to the soup kitchen and day shelters, sir? My vote would be for the kitchen. The other housing seems to be longer term. Also, I don't think there's any need to check out women's shelters, do you?"

"One step at a time sounds good," Gleason agreed.

"It would be nice if we had someone at KOTS or the soup kitchen," Powers said. "You know, to keep an eye open."

"You've played your undercover card," Gleason said. "The lieutenant won't approve any more. He's become a budget wonk."

"I know," Powers said ruefully. "I shouldn't have gone to Duval."

Gleason grinned.

"I might have a recruit," he said. "Let me think on it. Okay?"

"What about the blood traces at the last scene?" she asked. "Anything back from the lab?"

"Nothing yet. I was hoping to find a jewelers mark on the charm but it's run-of-the mill. Gold-plated, too. You can buy 'em at any shop."

"Maybe the engraving is special?"

"I ran that past a friend at a store in town. Standard issue."

"Apparently it was special to Keith, whoever that is."

~~~

A dead man in Phoenix bought a bus ticket to Miami. According to the station agent there, it had been sold to Benny Spring. Although it'd been a cash transaction, they required identification nonetheless, he'd added. Mr. Spring had produced a driver's license.

What an amazing piece of information, Dalton thought. This was radioactive stuff. She was at her desk in Van Nuys and had just finished speaking with the agent's supervisor.

There was no doubt in her mind that the deceased in question was a very much alive Leonard Hall. But why had he gone to Phoenix to catch a bus to Miami? Perhaps he thought that would give him some kind of cover. Especially if he'd been responsible for Benny's death. Fits the revenge hypotheses. Benny, then a bad joke on Wardel, and now off to Florida.

The evidence pointed to him. He was at the scene. He had Spring's credit card. Probably took his wallet. What about the gun? Maybe that, too.

So now he's a person of interest in a suspicious death, in possession of stolen property and possibly armed.

Most troubling is Miami. Just up the island chain from Key West and Jack Hunter.

There was only one thing she could do. She picked up her phone and dialed Hollywood.

"Detective Croaker, this is Laura Dalton."

"Good morning, detective. You caught me on my way out."

"I have some information on Benny Spring."

"Ah, well, I'm sure you have but Mr. Spring has been declared a suicide. That case is closed."

Dalton hadn't expected this.

"I think you might want to reopen it," she said.

"Detective, maybe Van Nuys has time on its hands but we're busier than hell in Hollywood. The Spring case is closed. Period. I suggest you stick to your own patch."

"Patch?" Dalton laughed. "You've been watching too many British detective shows. Tell you what, I'll email you what I have. And I'm serious about reopening that case. You really should hear what I've found out..."

"Nice talking with you," he snapped and hung up.

Dalton pondered Croaker's behavior. Why was he so adamant about the case being closed?

One of the detectives on the robbery table came in.

"Hey, what about that 187 in Hollywood yesterday?" he said. "Sicko, huh?"

One-eighty-seven is the California penal code for murder.

"I didn't hear about it," Dalton told him. "Been up to my neck lately."

"Yeah, when's Bradshaw due back from that homicide pow-wow in Palm Springs? Don't envy him. Must be unbearably hot down there."

"He spends all day in an air-conditioned meeting room so he's not suffering. His calendar says he should be here tomorrow," Dalton said. "Tell me about Hollywood."

"High-profile thing. TV star in town from New York picked up what he thought was a female prostitute on Sunset. Took her to his hotel. Turned out she was a he. Guy goes berserk and beats the fellow to death."

"That's terrible," Dalton said. "Who was it?"

"Under wraps right now. Network lawyers are trying to keep the asshole's name out of the papers until they can get a handle on it. Hollywood's being coy. Case will probably be kicked downtown like with OJ anyway."

Often high profile or celebrity investigations are taken over by the Robbery Homicide Unit, centered at police headquarters.

Dalton smiled to herself. Hollywood's homicide d-three is basking in Palm Springs. Big-time case pops up. Croaker closes the Spring investigation. Makes himself available for a nice slice of publicity if things go his way. The little star-fucker.

She wondered if the Benny Spring case really had been closed or was he just shining her on. Either way, he was willing to let an ongoing investigation of a possible homicide die on the vine for his personal gain. A pernicious man.

She began composing an email to Croaker, beginning with how sorry she was that Benny Spring had been declared a suicide and hoped that her information wasn't too late to reopen the investigation. Then she launched into everything she had discovered to date, including the bus ticket bought by 'Benny' and ending with her concern for Jack Hunter.

She copied Detective Bob Moyer and hit the send button, pulling the pin on a virtual hand grenade.

~~~

The tide neared its lowest mark, exposing the entire bank but leaving no sign of the missing charm. Maybe a damn fish picked it up. Or it didn't fall into the water. He searched the ground again leading back almost to the path. Nothing.

It was heartbreaking to have lost that. He should leave this place now. He might've been seen. There was still crime scene tape up by the road. The police could drive past any time and stop. He turned back toward the inlet once more, eyes on the ground. Hopeful.

The charm had been given in thanks. Not just a keepsake but a reminder that he'd been right to sacrifice everything to make a dream come true. Yet not three weeks later that dream had been shattered. The old routine put back on its track and wearisome as ever. And then, the frightening inevitable outcome. There was no fairness. But there *was* retribution.

He'd reached the water's edge. The tide had ebbed. He renewed the search.

Chapter 32

The bus pulled into the 27th Street station twelve hours behind schedule. The delay meant nothing to Leonard. He was in Miami. That was all that mattered.

He did have one concern, however. That nosy reporter at the accident scene was worrisome. Even more so was the cameraman. What if the pictures ended up on national television? He'd bet they would. A mile of wreckage, fatalities, busload of survivors. You couldn't ask for a better news story.

Glad to be off the bus, he went to look for a taxi. A stand was just down from the bus station.

"I'm going to Key West," he told the driver, jumping into the back seat.

"Which airline?" he said, driving off.

"No, not the airport. Key West."

The driver pulled over.

"You saying you want me to take you to Key West?"

"Yes."

"I have to call my wife. Tell her I'll be late."

Leonard had never been to Miami. Like some people who've never been to the west coast think Hawaii sets about thirty miles off California, he'd put Key West in Biscayne Bay.

"Be a round-trip charge," the driver said. "No meter."

"Uh, how much?"

"With the gas and all, six bills."

"Six hundred dollars? How far is it to Key West?"

"Little over a hundred miles down the keys. Takes four hours or so. Depending on traffic. I do three bucks a mile. Add it up. Sure you don't want the airport?"

Leonard had expected an anonymous taxi ride across town, now it was turning into an expedition. No, he didn't want to risk the airport. Too much security around and he didn't want anyone looking inside his bag.

"Do you take credit cards?" he asked.

"Yeah. But I have to charge it before we go, okay?"

Leonard handed the driver Benny Spring's card and leaned back in the seat. The taxi pulled away a minute later.

~~~

Bobby Sunshine gently backed the *Joyful Noise* into its new slip at Key West Bight. Jack stood on the dock watching.

"Grab ahold that line and tie me off," Bobby shouted from the open pilothouse door.

The boat secured, Bobby shut down the engine.

"Cost an arm and a leg to dock here," he grumbled. "All these big-ass boats running up the price everywhere you go. Damn fleets of the things. People showing off how rich they are, that's what."

"Why'd you leave Stock Island?" Jack asked. "Got to be cheaper there."

"Kicked me out of my space for some snowbird bringing down his yacht. Whole Island's gone to hell if you ask me."

Jack had earlier gotten a call from Bobby telling him to meet him at the Bight. That he was moving the boat to a new slip there. It was all very mysterious.

"Come aboard and let me show you the old scow," Bobby said.

Jack threw a leg over the side and stepped onto the aft deck. It brought back a memory of the night he'd first set foot on Astrid Kelly's sailboat. A night that began with a promise of romance and ended with a gun stuck up his nose.

"I extended the cabin to back here. Where you're standing used to be the work area for pulling in crab pots and nets. Let's go inside."

The doorway opened to a salon completely paneled with highly polished wood. Everything fitted as if done by a cabinetmaker. Ahead were steps up to the pilothouse, which had every navigational device imaginable, and another short stairwell leading down to the forward sleeping quarters. A comfortable place to snooze while plying away the nautical miles.

"This is fantastic, Bobby. You did all of it yourself?"

"I was once a carpenter," he winked.

"It's beautiful."

"You know how Ruth is. If we were going to see the world, I had to make things as homey as possible for her."

"Well, I'm sure she's pleased."

"How about a beer, Jack?"

"Be great."

Bobby got a couple of cans from the refrigerator in the galley.

"Here's to the Joyful Noise," Jack toasted. "And to smooth sailing for you and Ruth."

Bobby lifted his beer.

"When do you think you'll be heading out?" Jack asked, taking the opportunity.

"Like to talk with you about that, Jack."

~~~

Detective Powers was stunned by the idea. Gleason waited for a response, a grin on his face. The two were driving south on North Roosevelt in Power's car. Traffic was heavy going both directions.

"You're suggesting we use Jack Hunter?" she asked.

"Can't think of a better person for the job," he told her.

She frowned.

"I don't know, sir. First, he's a civilian. What if something happens? And then I'm not all that sure how reliable he is. You, yourself, have had misgivings. Just the other day you were considering him as a possible suspect. I know that's different now but still."

"Hunter can handle himself," Gleason said gruffly. "All I'm talking about is him keeping his eyes and ears open. This isn't secret agent stuff. Back to his having been a suspect, I never did think he had anything to do with these murders. I told you that."

Powers shook her head. She wasn't convinced that Jack Hunter was that great a choice for undercover but she wasn't going to push it.

"The department could be setting itself up for a lawsuit," she argued instead. "Wouldn't it be better to use a sworn officer?"

"I appreciate your concerns, Rachel. Hunter was once homeless. He can relate."

"That still doesn't answer why we shouldn't use one of ours. A good cop can relate as well as a former homeless."

"Hunter has something more in his favor. He was afraid of the police when he was on the run, so to speak. He can understand how some of the homeless feel. A little empathy goes a long way."

"Empathy doesn't do much if he gets hurt and decides to sue," she said.

"That wouldn't be a thing Hunter would do," Gleason said.

Powers gave up.

"If you say so, sir. You believe our bad guy works at the soup kitchen?"

"No, not necessarily. But he could be a regular there. Or knows the place."

They passed over the bridge across the inlet to the Blue Bayou. Up ahead traffic had come to a complete stop, backed up from the signal light at the intersection. Powers glanced into the rearview mirror as she braked.

"Sir, someone just came up from below the bridge," she said excitedly.

Gleason spun around to look out the back window. He saw a male figure begin to walk away.

"Make a U-turn!" he shouted.

"I can't, sir. Traffic's too bad."

Gleason opened the passenger door and jumped out. He began running on the center line back toward the bridge. Powers flashed her headlights repeatedly and laid on the horn as she edged out of her lane and into the oncoming traffic.

The man turned in a hotel driveway and disappeared from view.

Gleason had miraculously managed to get across the boulevard without being hit and had reached the bridge when Powers stopped beside him.

"Keep going," he puffed, winded. "He went down that next driveway."

Powers raced ahead and swung into the drive. She drove past the hotel entrance and circled the parking lot. There was no one to be seen. She continued around to the back of the building and out to the entrance again.

Gleason met her there.

"Nothing," she said. "Did you get a look at what he was wearing?"

"Shirt and shorts is all I know. I'm going inside. You stay here in case he comes out."

Gleason returned a few minutes later.

"Nobody noticed anything," he said. "Guests come and go all day. Pool's full of people. Could be there or anywhere."

"Should we go back to the bridge?"

"I don't know what for but why not? Leave the car. We'll walk."

~~~

The person they were hoping to find had cut through a small stand of trees to the grounds of an adjacent hotel. He now sat in its lobby perusing a newspaper.

"Are you waiting for the shuttle, sir?"

The man looked up.

"Right out front," the shuttle driver said. "We're leaving in five minutes."

"Where do you stop in town?"

"Simonton and Green. Everybody gets off there. Same place for the return."

He followed the driver out.

~~~

Powers and Gleason had scrambled down the path at the base of the bridge.

"Maybe the guy had to take a leak, that was all." Gleason said, looking around.

"You'd think the yellow tape would've kept him out."

"Depends on how bad he had to go," Gleason laughed.

"I'm not so sure, sir. He could've gone to the restroom at the hotel. I believe he was here looking for something."

"Maybe," Gleason nodded. "Or just morbid curiosity or whatever causes people to return to the scene of their crime."

Powers stood at the water's edge.

"Like that gold charm we found right at this spot," she said insistently.

"That sure is a possibility, Rachel. I wish we could identify the damn thing. My guy said they were a dime a dozen. Well, maybe a little more than that but still a pretty common item."

"Nothing noteworthy about the engraving, right?"

"Yeah, your basic lettering, nothing fancy. And the other thing is we don't know if it was even bought in Key West."

"The message was important, though. Whoever had it done was probably very particular that it be just right. Might've taken a lot of time deciding. Someone might remember that. How many jewelry shops are in town?"

"Christ, I don't know," Gleason shrugged. "Some have been around forever, others come and go as fast as t-shirt shops."

"I'd like to put together a list of all the jewelry stores both in town and in the shopping centers and show that charm to them."

Gleason bunched his lips and nodded.

"Let's head back to the station."

Chapter 33

Lugo Croaker's nervous system was popping. Anger and fear had collided head-on, leaving all circuits fried. He read the email once more.

"That bothersome bitch," he muttered through locked teeth.

It was time for some damage control before Moyer got back. He picked up his phone to call Dalton but hesitated. What was he going to say? He couldn't just ream her out for sticking her nose in. That wasn't going to fly anymore. She had real evidence now. Work that should've had his name on it. Then he remembered the credit card statement Spring's secretary had told him about. He scrolled to her number and called. Luckily, the woman answered.

"Detective Croaker, nice to hear from you."

"Yes, ma'am, how is everything going with you?"

"We're closing the office tomorrow," she said sadly. "Packed the last box."

"Well, I suppose that's good. What I'm calling about is that credit statement you mentioned. Have there been any more charges?"

"I don't know. I was waiting a few days before closing the account. Also, I guess I would need a death certificate for poor Mister Spring."

"Could you fax me the last statement? The one you initially called about?"

"Of course. I'll do it right away."

Croaker gave her the fax number.

"Don't do anything about closing the account just yet, ma'am. And don't worry about that death certificate. I'll check on it and get back to you."

And he'd also be checking with the fraud department at the credit company, he thought to himself. Get that list. Head off any trouble before it landed at his desk. No way was Detective Laura Dalton going to undermine him.

~~~

"How about another beer, Jack?"

"Still working on this one, Bobby."

That was the third beer the old man had downed. Jack wondered what was up.

"Well, don't fall too far behind me, son."

Bobby pulled another can from the refrigerator, snapped it open and returned to his seat.

"Guess I've worked up enough Dutch courage," he said, looking Jack straight in the eyes. "Might as well come clean."

"My God, what is it?" Jack asked.

"Ruth's not a well woman."

Jack reached over and placed a hand on Bobby's shoulder.

"Is it serious?"

"She doesn't think so. She wouldn't, of course. But I believe it's her heart."

Jack nodded, saying nothing.

"Been having chest pains," Bobby said. "Usually right after eating. That doesn't sound right to me."

"Has she seen a doctor?"

"Doesn't believe in them."

"How long has it been going on?"

"For some time. I looked it up on the internet. Heart attacks, that sort of thing. Big killer among women. Most people don't know that."

Jack went over to the galley and opened the refrigerator.

"Think I'll join you with that beer."

Bobby finished his and crushed the can in his hand.

"I didn't want to make this trip," he said. getting up and going to the refrigerator himself, "but Ruth wouldn't hear of it. She can be pretty stubborn when she takes a mind."

"She's got to see a doctor," Jack said.

"I know it. You know it. She won't."

"What can I do? Tell me."

"I don't think we should leave Key West right now," Bobby said, shaking his head. "Something happened coming down, I could get to a hospital. Out in the middle of the ocean's another story."

"Sounds reasonable to me."

"Yeah, reasonable to anyone else but we're talking about Ruth LaVere. The only thing that might keep her here is Roy."

"Oh, she'll listen to him?"

"Roy wasn't a happy bird on the boat. A seagull came aboard on the Pamlico Sound and stayed until we were past Wilmington. Perched on the aft deck squawking half the day. Upsetting as all hell to Roy. Couldn't shoo the damn thing away. It'd just circle the boat and come right back."

Jack couldn't help but smile at that. However, this was serious business.

"Then poor Roy never did get his sea legs. By the time we hit Florida, I was thinking of stopping to look for a vet. About then he started to perk up some. Must've been the Florida air. Reminded him of home, you know."

"He seemed to be in good spirits when I last saw him," Jack said.

"Absolutely," Bobby said. "That's because he's back on dry land. And don't think Ruth hasn't noticed, either."

Jack was beginning to see where all this might be going.

"Has Ruth also perked up some since getting back?" he asked.

"I believe so. Got more energy. Hasn't had any dizzy spells like when she was on the boat. Eating better, too, since Derrick started doing the cooking."

Jack sat quiet for a moment. Then he leaned toward Bobby.

"Ruth wants her house back and she sent you to tell me, is that right?"

Bobby's face flushed. Jack wasn't sure it was from embarrassment or the beer.

"I was just getting around to that, Jack. See, we could make a trade. What would you think of living here? On this boat?"

Now Jack did have to laugh aloud.

"She's a fine craft," Bobby said, ignoring him. "Had her completely refitted. You could hire a captain and take her out any time. Hell, I'll captain it for you. Dock fee wouldn't be any more than you're paying for rent now. And you'd be doing Ruth a big favor. And me, too. For looking after this boat. I don't have to tell you that, son."

Jack paid Bobby a long, even look.

"Guess we should have a beer to celebrate my new digs," he said.

Chapter 34

Bobby had hooked up the dock's electrical power and water lines and then given Jack another more thorough tour of the *Joyful Noise,* explaining every last thing about the boat twice, before saying his goodbyes.

Jack promised he'd drop by the house later to pick up the rest of his stuff. During the walkthrough, he'd noticed that there was not a stitch of Bobby's or Ruth's belongings on board. He had smiled to himself at that. The deal had been settled before the talk began. No doubt the old guy had been stretching the story concerning Ruth's heart issues. Closer to the truth would be that she wasn't taken by the seafaring life.

After Bobby had left, he'd remained on board getting a feel for his new home and letting the fact sink in that he no longer lived in the old one that he'd come to know so well. And yes, love.

He'd certainly been taken aback by the whole business. And he would rather have had Ruth tell him in person that he was being kicked out instead of sending Bobby to do the job.

Jesus H. Christ, he thought. First, they land in on him vague as all hell about how long they planned to stay. Next thing, he has to move to a damn motel so Derrick can keep his room. Not very fair, if you asked him.

The house had always been Ruth's, though. He was just a tenant. Then and there and now here.

Even in LA, for all practical purposes. And why was that? He owned the beach house in Malibu yet had never really considered it his home. Always temporary lodging, as far as he was concerned. A place to stay when in town. Same as with the apartment he'd bought there. He could buy a great little house in Key West. On a terrific block in Old Town. But he knew he wouldn't. There was just something about permanence that'd always put him off.

Well, being a live-aboard in Key West Bight might not be all that bad. He would need to get a few things, starting with new linens. There weren't any. He wrote a list.

Finally, he locked up and walked down the dock, turning to look at the boat once more before heading over to Duval Street.

He'd passed Caroline when he noticed a man leaving a jewelry store ahead of him.

"Hey, Mike," he called out.

Mike Galvin turned around.

"Thought it was you," Jack said, catching up. "Jack Hunter, from the soup kitchen."

"Of course. I'm sorry. Had my mind elsewhere."

"Going up town? I'll walk with you."

"Actually, I'm heading the other way."

With a smile and a finger wave, Mike did an about-face and left him standing there. Jack watched as he disappeared around the corner. He couldn't decide if the guy was rude or just another Key West joker. A car pulled over on the opposite side of the street and honked its horn. Jack looked to see its driver lowering the window.

"Hunter," Gleason yelled. "Come here."

Jack waited until a pack of motor scooters had passed and then darted across Duval.

"Get in," Gleason said.

"Where's your sidekick?" Jack asked, slipping into the front passenger seat.

"Detective Powers is busy."

"So what's this? Boys' night out?"

"I'm busy, too."

Jack nodded and waited to hear what was next, but

Gleason said nothing. He turned off Duval and crossed over several streets before finally parking by a short lane. Salty Dick's stood at its end.

"Your girlfriend still work at this dump?" he asked, getting out of the car.

"If you mean Nora, I don't know. Haven't been here for awhile."

When Jack first arrived in Key West, he'd lived with Nora and her boyfriend, Brownie. It had been a mercurial relationship among the three of them.

Salty Dick's was a late-night venue for local musicians but it was early yet, and the place was empty when the two men entered. Nora wasn't tending bar.

"Great day for drinking, guys" the barman said.

"Couple of beers," Gleason told him. "Okay if we take 'em over to a table?"

"Sure. Sit any place you like."

"Didn't I use to see you at the little Tiki?" Jack asked. "Steve, right?"

"Yeah, I fill in here once in awhile."

"Nora still around?"

"She moved up to Destin."

Jack and Gleason settled at a spot in the corner. The barman changed channels on the TV. Golf match somewhere in Florida.

"I've been thinking about the soup kitchen," Gleason said.

"If there's an opening, I can put in a word."

Gleason leaned forward.

"I expect you to keep this to yourself, Hunter. I'm serious. Not a word. You understand?"

Jack nodded that he did.

"These homeless murders," Gleason continued. "I feel one person's behind them. Probably a male and not homeless himself but involved with them. And he targets his victims."

"I won't ask how you know all this but why are you telling me?" Jack asked.

"He could be you."

Jack leaned back.

"Here we go again," he said. "You people are conspiracy theorists, you know that?"

Jack got up from the table.

"Let me explain," Gleason said. "Then you can leave."

Jack reluctantly sat down.

"You're a volunteer for the homeless services," Gleason said. "Our suspect could also be one."

"And?"

"And you might be able to help us find him. We can check out employees and volunteers at the shelters and houses, but I don't believe he's there. Our man is playing some kind of game. He's selective about his victims."

"So you're thinking he's using the soup kitchen for his...?"

"It's a busy place. People come and go. Lots of choices."

A crazy thought jumped into Jack's head.

"Are you asking me to play the role of a homeless person?" he asked. "So this maniac could, what, hit on me?"

"Actually, I had something else in mind but that's not a bad idea. No, keep doing whatever you're doing now. Anything you think we ought to know, don't be shy about telling us."

Jack thought that over.

"In other words you're asking me to be a snitch," he said.

"That's one word for it, I suppose. Little dramatic, though."

"I don't like the sound of it."

"How about observer? That's a nicer word."

"Suppose I screw up? Get someone in trouble over

nothing. Happens all the time."

"We won't let it happen. This would only be for information. Something to investigate further. Up to you, Hunter. Yes or no and we're out of here."

"I'm moving," Jack said. "Need some time to gather up my things."

"Oh, yeah? Where to."

"A boat in Key West Bight."

"One of those big jobs? Must've set you back."

"Commercial fishing boat. I just swapped places with my landlady."

"Guess you know a deal when you see one."

Chapter 35

"You want to stop for a cup of coffee, Mr. Spring? Restaurant right up ahead."

The taxi had just driven into Matecumbe Key. They'd left the last remnants of daylight passing through Key Largo. Now it was completely dark.

"How much farther before Key West?"

"Well, Marathon's not too far down the road. Another hour after that."

"Yeah, let's stop. I need to take a leak."

A single car was parked out front. They pulled in next to it.

"Doesn't look busy," the driver said, as they entered.

"Hi, gents," a woman greeted. "The kitchen's about to close."

"Get a couple of coffees to go?" the driver asked.

"I'm hitting the head," Leonard said.

"It's around the side, honey," the woman said. "Here's the key."

"Maybe two pieces of that key lime pie in the case," the driver pointed.

"Sure thing. Where you boys coming from?"

"Miami. Going to Key West."

"Must be one humdinger of a taxi fare's all I can say," she laughed.

The restroom was clean, if small. At least he didn't have to worry about some big con checking him out, sizing him up. Taking him for his bitch. He emptied his bladder and zipped up his jeans.

"Here's your key," Leonard said, coming back inside.

"Thanks, honey. Enjoy Key West."

Outside, he turned to the driver.

"What the hell did you tell her?"

"She asked where we were going," the driver shrugged. "Taxi caught her attention, that's all."

Yeah, enough to make her remember. He should dump this idiot off a bridge and take the car. Too bad the credit card had been run. Right now all anyone knows is that Benny Spring is in Miami. Not that the cops are going to figure anything out anytime soon. He'll always be three steps ahead of them. Still, it would've been better to have paid cash. Stay totally off the grid. Maybe there's a way to make this guy and his car disappear. Something to think about over the next hour.

"Let's go," he said roughly.

~~~

Jack had asked Gleason to drop him off at Stella by Starlight after their meeting at Salty Dick's. He wanted to talk with Derrick. It was a slow night and a sudden rain shower had emptied Duval Street.

"I don't know what to say, Jack."

They were sitting inside the restaurant. Rain was still dripping on the patio.

"It's where *you* live, man!" Derrick argued. "I realize Ruth's the owner and all. But I can't just barge in there and take your place."

"Look at it this way. I've already agreed to move on the boat. That's where I live now and I think it's going to be fun. The other thing is you'd be doing me a favor by staying at the house."

Derrick shifted in his chair which creaked for mercy under the weight.

"They're getting old and need someone around," Jack continued. "Bobby's full of bluster, as you've probably noticed, and Ruth is contrary as ever. They won't admit to needing anything, of course. But you'd be there. You'd be the caretaker, so to speak. More importantly, a voice of reason. Believe me on that last part."

"Billy mentioned me moving in with him. Work's completed at his house."

"That'd certainly be your choice. I don't know how much rent Billy would charge. He'd be pretty fair about it, though."

"Rent? He's my uncle. Why would he charge me anything?"

"This is Key West, Derrick, no space goes unrented. Unwritten law. Bobby think's you're my tenant. I expect he'll soon be wanting to know what you pay. Make up a figure. I'll see to it that it's added to the monthly."

"That's not fair, Jack. I can't let you do that. What do you mean 'monthly'?"

"I rent the house now through a realtor who sends it on to Ruth. I'm going to continue paying it. Ruth doesn't have all that much income, so it'll help. I'll just bump up the amount. Tell Bobby that's how it works in Florida. State law or something. Has to come through a rental agent. He'll be happy."

"What about Roy? Who's going to read to him? He's not crazy about me."

"I'll drop by every now and then."

~~~

Dalton's telephone rang.

"Van Nuys homicide. This is Detective Dalton."

It was nearly seven o'clock in the evening. The detective's room was empty save for a couple of officers still at their desks.

"Glad to catch you in, detective. Afraid you might be out somewhere having cocktails."

She recognized Croaker's voice.

"I'm busy, Detective Croaker. If you're lonesome at your bar, call someone else."

"Actually, I'm also at the office. I read your little email."

"Happy to hear that. Hope it helps."

"Oh, I think you have another hope in mind. Exactly what kind of crap are you trying to pull off, Dalton?"

"I don't understand, Detective Croaker. Crap?"

"You know exactly what I'm talking about. You'd better watch your step or else you might be in for a big fall, sweetheart."

Dalton signaled for one of the other detectives to pick up on her extension. He grabbed his phone and punched her extension.

"Are you threatening me, Detective Croaker?"

"Now why would I need to do something silly like that?"

Dalton looked over at the detective and nodded.

"I don't know," she said. "Sounded like a threat. You tell me."

"Just consider this a heads-up, detective. Otherwise you might get your head handed to you. My advice would be stay out of Hollywood's business."

"I'm trying to," Dalton said. "That's why I sent you the email. You told me that the Benny Spring case had been declared a suicide and closed. I have since discovered information that could effect that decision. I turned it over to you as requested by your detective three. So what is your problem?"

"I never said the case was closed. What gave you that idea?"

Dalton closed her eyes. She should've seen that one coming.

"In fact, we're very much aware of the credit card charges made after Mr. Spring's death," Croaker said. "I've spoken with his secretary about them. All part of our ongoing investigation."

"Then you must be aware of the danger placed on Jack Hunter by Leonard Hall."

Croaker gave a derisive snort.

"Three points, detective," he said. "Listen carefully. Point number one, we haven't identified Hall as being involved. Two, all we *do* have is that Benny Spring's credit card is being used by someone, possibly whoever found his billfold. Three, your Jack Hunter has nothing to do with this case."

Dalton took in a breath.

"There's a fourth point, Croaker. And that is you're missing the whole point. There's no question in my mind that Hall was in that building on the day Benny allegedly jumped. I know the little shit and I know what he's capable of doing. As far as whoever *found* that billfold goes, I guarantee you it was Leonard. He also apparently found the money in the cash box and Benny's gun."

"Hey, detective," Croaker laughed. "You once accused me of watching too many British detective shows, I think you've become hooked on CSI."

"This isn't funny, detective," Dalton said. "Leonard Hall bought a bus ticket to Miami for one reason only. To find Jack Hunter. He's after revenge."

"I thought you said your lover was in Key West. Isn't that somewhere else?"

She started to tell this creep that Jack wasn't her lover but decided not to give him the pleasure of knowing that he'd gotten to her.

"Maybe that's as far as the bus goes," Dalton said. "I don't know. Maybe he'll rent a car in Miami and drive the rest of the way. One more thing. I believe the reason he took a bus instead of flying is that he's armed. Benny Spring's gun? The one you apparently aren't concerned about? Tough to get a gun through TSA."

"You know, detective, you should get out of this business. With that mind of yours, you could make a fortune writing television shows. Have a good evening."

Dalton put down her phone.

"He's lying," she said to the other detective.

He was also, she realized, very clever. Good at this game. Yes, she had better watch her step if she was going to continue to play.

"You know this guy Croaker?" the detective asked.

"We go back."

~~~

"This is Boca Chica we're passing through," the driver said. "Big navy air station here. Stock Island's next and then Key West. What hotel are you staying at?"

"Don't have one."

That was an unpleasant surprise. He hadn't thought about a hotel. Well, why should he have? If Key West had been where it was supposed to be in Miami, he wouldn't have been there long enough to need a hotel. He would've gone straight to Jack Hunter's home, taken care of business and been on his way. Instead, he was in a crummy taxi riding to who the hell knows where.

"It's off-season," the driver said. "Shouldn't be hard to find a room."

"Got a recommendation?"

"Hang on and I'll look on my phone."

Good thing he'd decided not to get rid of this jerk, he thought. Another smart move on his part.

"There's a DoubleTree the other side of the bridge. This time of year they're wide open."

The driver hadn't bothered checking for vacancies. The sooner he dumped this turkey the better.

They crossed the little bridge separating Stock Island and Key West and turned left onto South Roosevelt. The hotel entrance came up quickly and the taxi pulled into its drive.

"Well, it's been a pleasure, Mr. Spring. Enjoy your stay in Key West."

"Yeah, wait here until I make sure they have a room."

"Yes, sir."

Leonard grabbed up his overnight bag and headed for the lobby. The taxi took off as soon as he was through the entrance door.

No one was inside. He rang a bell on the counter and a moment later the night clerk appeared from around the corner.

"May I help you?"

"I'd like a room."

"I'm sorry, sir, but the hotel is full at the present. We have a writer's conference."

"Don't hand me that bullshit," he said angrily. "Every hotel keeps an extra room or so available. Just in case."

"I'm afraid not this time, sir. Not even a broom closet."

"Can you call another hotel then?"

"The town's pretty busy. I know there's nothing available at this end of the island. Our shuttle has stopped running for the evening but I can call a taxi to take you down- town. You might find something there."

"Don't go to any trouble, asshole," he snapped. "I have a taxi waiting."

He stomped out of the lobby only to find an empty space waiting.

Now he was sorry that he hadn't killed the stupid driver and taken the car. Well, be damned if he would go back inside and beg that little prick to call him a cab. He'd walk to downtown. Couldn't be all that far.

An hour later and three tiring miles from the DoubleTree, he'd settled on a park bench near Garrison Bight for a short rest.

Dawn had neared half-light when the KWPD cruiser stopped at curbside.

"Hey, partner," the lone officer shouted, stepping out of the car. "Wake up!"

Leonard roused himself and got to his feet.

"Sorry, officer, I was taking a late-night walk and sat down for just a minute. Must've dozed off."

"C'mere," the cop ordered.

Leonard walked over to him, leaving his overnight bag on the bench.

"You got some identification?" he asked, giving him a once-over.

Leonard was dressed in a pair of jeans and a light jacket. The clothes looked new and clean. Definitely not the usual homeless getup.

"Sure," he said. "Okay if I reach in my back pocket for my wallet?"

"Turn around," he ordered, all business and meaning it. "Get down on your knees, hands in the air."

Leonard complied. A pair of cuffs was slapped on him.

"Now stand up."

Leonard stood, not saying a word. The officer appeared to be nervous.

"The reason I'm restraining you, sir, is for both of our safety. Your wallet's in which pocket?"

"The right."

He removed the wallet and flipped it open.

"Okay, turn around and face me. Slowly."

The officer scrutinized the license photo.

"Benjamin Spring," he read. "From Los Angeles. Not a very good picture, sir."

"You should see my passport," Leonard joked.

The cop smiled.

"Vacationing?" he asked.

"I'm here for the writer's conference," Leonard said.

The officer nodded and removed the handcuffs.

"What kind of books do you write?"

"I write movie scripts," Leonard said, rubbing his wrists. "Westerns."

"Really? Have I seen any of your movies?"

"They're mostly for foreign audiences."

He was so good at this, he thought. Stupid fucking cop.

"Thank you, Mr. Spring," the officer said, returning the wallet. "Sorry for the inconvenience. We've had a number of violent crimes in this area. I recommend you skip taking those late-night walks."

"Thank you, officer. I'll use the experience in my next script."

"Have a good day, sir."

Leonard watched him drive away. Sucker, he thought.

Chapter 36

Jack had also gotten an early start to the day. After checking out of the Straits Motel, he'd walked to the Key West Bight parking lot where he'd left his scooter the evening before. From there he'd ridden out to the shopping center and bought the things he needed to finish furnishing the *Joyful Noise*. By midmorning his new home was, well, shipshape.

He relaxed with a cup of coffee on the small afterdeck. A couple of tarpons rose to the water's surface, then like spent torpedoes, sank to the bottom. One of the large catamarans berthed nearby glided past on its way out of the harbor, its deck alive with snorkelers. Tourists leisurely strolled along the boardwalk, occasionally stopping for a photo. Morning was always best at the Bight.

He should call Billy. Poor guy didn't know he had moved. He pulled out his phone and punched speed dial.

"Jack," Billy answered. "How's living on the water again working for you, hee-hee?"

Small island, Jack thought. Nothing goes unnoticed.

"Yes, sir," Billy continued. "Derrick said the boss lady there kicked you out and now he's the man of the house. That so?"

"Every word of it is true," Jack laughed.

"Think you're a good person for moving out like that," Billy said. "Folks wanted to be in their place, that's all. Good for letting Derrick stay on, too."

"Sorry to beat you out of a rental," Jack said, "but it's a help having him there to keep an eye on things. Look, I'm volunteering at the soup kitchen this afternoon, so I won't see you until later."

"Got you covered, Jack. Slow all over town anyway. Decided to close Stella by Starlight one night a week."

"Probably wise thing to do. Oh, I forgot to ask. We have anyone playing tonight?"

"That guitar fellow was supposed to show up but he's sick. Hope one of those mosquitos didn't bite him. I burn a citrus candle every night to keep 'em away."

"That oughta do it, Billy. Anyway I've got an idea for some music tonight."

Jack hung up and made another call.

"This is Jewel. I can't get to the phone. Leave your name and number..."

He hung up before the beep, deciding to just call later. Hopefully, the Flamin' Flamingos aren't already booked.

~~~

Leonard stood at the corner of Truman and Duval. The sun had suddenly gotten serious about the day and the only breeze came from the passing traffic. He'd stuffed his jacket in the bag but all that did was add weight. The .40 Sig Sauer packed at the bottom didn't help, either.

This must be the center of town, he figured, given the crowded sidewalks. So far he wasn't impressed. Also, he'd noticed a number of police cars patrolling. Problem for anyone living on the street, if his earlier experience was any indication. He really needed to find somewhere to stay.

He joined a group of tourists meandering down Duval. A few steps later, they'd stopped in front of a guesthouse to take pictures and he took the opportunity to duck into the office.

"Hello," a woman seated at a desk greeted. "May I help you?"

"Yes, I was interested in a room."

"Well, we're pretty much full but I do have one available. Is it just for you?"

"The one and only," he smiled.

"It's small and by the pool."

"That's okay. How much?"

"Three-forty-nine, including the tax."

"I only need it for one night."

"That is for one night."

It wasn't that he couldn't pay. There was the credit card, although he was starting to feel a little nervous about using it. What if they were tracing the charges? Counting what he'd taken from Benny and the ATMs, he certainly had enough cash on him. But he had other plans for that money when he'd finished here.

"It sounds really nice," he sighed, 'but to be honest, I'm on a strict budget. Is there somewhere you could recommend that might be more...it's kind of embarrassing."

The woman came to his rescue.

"Try Crackers Court. It's on Lester Lane. I'll give you a map. Wait a sec. Let me call them first."

He smiled inward. He could charm the birds out of the trees.

~~~

Detective Three Tom Bradshaw sat silently for a full minute while Detective Two Laura Dalton died a thousand deaths across from him at the homicide desk. At last he spoke.

"What were you thinking, Laura?"

It was Bradshaw's first day back and Dalton had filled him in on the Benny Spring case, including showing him the email she'd sent to Hollywood.

"You can't take over an investigation in another division. My God, Laura, you could be up before the board for this! Possibly lose your job!"

"I'm not trying to take over anything," she said firmly. "I spoke with Detective Moyer. He told me to email him and Detective Croaker what I had."

"But why were you involved at all?"

"I had this feeling."

"Perhaps you'd like to explain that."

"Came from a string of coincidences, I guess. Leonard Hall being released from prison. His behavior during the trial. Benny Spring's alleged suicide. Something just clicked, I don't know. When I saw Leonard on the security camera, it all made a crazy kind of sense."

"But not to the investigating detective at Hollywood."

"I can't answer that. I know what Hall looks like."

"That doesn't give you the right to go over the detective's head."

"I didn't take it any further until I saw the television news story. Then I thought I knew what Leonard Hall was up to."

"All speculation, Laura."

"No, Tom, a hunch."

"So now you've taken your *hunch* to the head of homicide at Hollywood."

"I wasn't certain Detective Croaker was following up. And actually it's more than just a feeling. I know Leonard Hall."

"Jesus Christ!" Bradshaw said, turning his head aside. "Listen to yourself."

"I was in the wrong," Dalton admitted. "Detective Moyer set me straight on that."

"And you just assumed the case was closed when, in fact, the investigating officer at Hollywood says it's open. What the hell's going on?"

"I don't know. And that's just it. Detective Croaker *did* say the case was closed."

Bradshaw took in a breath and exhaled.

"Well, apparently there's some disagreement about that," he said.

"Croaker told me the case was closed. I didn't make it up, Tom. And what about Leonard Hall's fingerprints on the key box? Remember? He stole the Lexus and drove it to Arizona. It's obvious. But no one wants to know. Especially, Croaker."

Bradshaw looked at her.

"Do you have a background with this Croaker?" he asked. "I mean, what's the problem here? Something going on between you two?"

Dalton blushed.

"You'd have to ask him that."

"Well, he could file a complaint with IA."

Croaker filing a complaint with internal affairs on her, she thought. How ironic.

"Tom, I'm certain that Leonard Hall is somehow involved with the death of Benny Spring. I believe he is now in Florida to harm someone I know. I can't just let that go. And if it costs me my job, I don't care."

"All right, calm down. I'll talk with Moyer. Meanwhile, stay out of Croaker's hair."

~~~

"There won't be lunch today," Sonja Lidman sadly announced to staff. "It seems our person in charge of shopping is out with the flu or whatever and didn't call to let us know until it was too late."

The little group was assembled in the kitchen. Jack had just joined them.

"They run this place like that?" he whispered to Mike Galvin. "Left hand doesn't tell the right?"

"Happens often," Galvin whispered back. "They shop irregularly. Supposed to buy enough food for three or four days at a time. Should get someone else for the job. This one they've got now is a real ding-a-ling."

Jack nodded. Maybe he could come up with a better plan. He'd mention it to Billy.

"I'm stepping outside for a smoke," Galvin said. "Want to join me?"

"Sure. It's just as well we have the rest of the day off. I can use the time."

"Busy, huh?" Galvin said, lighting up and offering the pack. "You still off cigarettes?"

Jack declined with a wave of his hand.

"Trying to but thanks anyway."

"So what're you doing that takes so much time?" Galvin asked.

"Moving to another place. About got everything under control. Few odds and ends, you know how it goes."

"Boy, do I ever. Say, didn't mean to blow you off when you ran into me on Duval. Just remembered I had to be somewhere."

"Done it myself many times," Jack laughed.

He noticed the injury to Galvin's neck.

"That looks kind of angry. Careful it doesn't get infected."

"Dumb accident," Galvin chuckled. "Nothing to worry about. So tell me again how did you come to volunteer."

"There was a time I was homeless. Got some help from strangers. Made a promise to return the favor someday. Here I am."

"Pretty noble of you," Galvin said, reaching for the string he wore around his neck and fingering the small charm attached to it.

"I also made a similar promise," he added.

~~~

Key West is a fine place for discovering. With its maize of right-angled streets in varying lengths and little lanes that suddenly submerge to surface elsewhere, you never know where you might end up.

Crackers Court was down a hidden alley five unequal blocks the other side of Duval. A tough enough walk even if you knew the way. Leonard, being new in town, had wandered off course several times even though he had a map, although one of so-so accuracy and scale. Finally, he turned in Lester Lane.

"You the person Sharron called about?" the girl behind the desk trilled. "She's so nice."

Leonard flopped down on a chair in the small area that served for an office.

"I'm Benny Spring."

"Welcome to Crackers Court, Mr. Spring. I'm Heather. Luckily, we do have one room left."

"I'll take it."

"Great!" Heather chirped. "Let me show you. It's right next to us."

She led him to a glass-fronted door that opened into what appeared to be a partitioned-off hallway.

"It's a little close. But since it's only yourself, you should be okay. Okay?"

"Is there a bathroom?"

"Behind the curtain."

Leonard dropped his bag on the folding bed and followed Heather back to the office.

"It's a hundred-forty-nine a night," Heather said, her finger on a calculator. "With taxes, uh, one-sixty-four. Okay?"

He handed her Benny's credit card. He'd soon be leaving this hellhole, so he'd decided to chance one more charge.

"How far is Ashe Street from here?" he asked.

"I'll give you a map."

Chapter 37

"It's a nice little charm," the salesman said. "Fourteen karat gold-plated. But not special. Nothing distinguishing, I mean."

"Not even the engraving?" Powers asked.

"Not really. Plain and simple lettering."

"Well, thank you for your time."

"Sorry I couldn't help."

She left the jewelry shop and got in her car to drive back to the police station. Gleason was in the detective room when she arrived.

"Nada," she said, taking a seat at the table. "It's the universal charm. Seen one, you've seen them all."

"Wonder if we should expand the search," Gleason said, biting his lower lip. "Maybe up to Marathon. What do you think?"

"Why stop there, sir? I can drive on up the east coast. Must be hundreds of jewelry stores in New York."

The frustration of not finding anything solid in the investigation was beginning to tell on both detectives. Sarcasm provided a small outlet.

"That the end of the list?" Gleason asked.

"No, a couple more on Duval Street. Just thought I'd start nearer the crime scenes, for no particular reason."

"Makes as much sense as anything else about this case."

"Any news from our informant?" Powers asked.

"Jack Hunter? No. I really don't expect much there."

"Maybe we should start over," Powers suggested. "Isn't that what you're supposed to do when you run out of ideas? Go back to the beginning?"

Gleason sat with the thought for a moment.

"All right, get out the murder books for each victim," he said. "We'll read them together."

"Richard Kirby first?"

"No, the one before him. The shooting at the beach."

~ ~ ~

Jack had dropped by Ashe Street to check on Bobby and Ruth. He rang the doorbell. It felt odd. Derrick answered.

"Hey, it's Jack. Come in, man."

Bobby looked up from the newspaper, grunted and went back to reading. Roy perched on the back of a chair fascinated by something. Ruth banged around in the kitchen. Home.

"Restaurant's closed tonight," Derrick said. "Billy says business should pick up once season starts."

Jack walked over to Roy and smoothed the feathers on his head.

"Yeah, Billy told me," he said. "So how's everything else going?"

"Moving right along. You settling into your new place?"

Small talk. Already he had become a stranger.

"Getting there," he said.

Ruth came in from the kitchen.

"Hello, Jack."

She gathered up Roy and put him in the cage.

"Thought I'd stop by for my things," Jack said.

"They're not in the way."

Jack shrugged.

"I'll just take the saxophone then," he said.

Ruth busied herself with Roy.

"I understand you're seeing Ruby Steele," she said, turning to Jack.

"I've seen her one time, Ruth. The day she got here."

She gave him a stern look.

"Just be careful with that poor girl."

So that was what was behind the peculiar behavior. She

still blamed him for Ruby's having to leave town. Well, maybe she should. Though he had only been trying to help then. But like they say about good deeds...

"I promise," he said, smiling and taking her hands in his.

"Jack," Bobby called out, laying aside the newspaper. "Derrick's cooking. Staying for dinner?"

"Got to be at Billy's tonight. Next time?"

The earth was back in its groove and all was right. How often it had seemed to get knocked off track lately.

~~~

Following the map on which Heather had drawn directions, Leonard came to Ashe Street. He stopped to rest in the shade beneath a small tree overhanging the sidewalk.

This was a dry run for him. Once he'd located the house, he would return later that night. Then tomorrow he'd be gone. Maybe back to Texas, who knows? The idea of writing that western appealed. He looked at a paper scrap he'd jotted the address on.

Odd numbers across the street, so the house should be on this side. Should only be four up from where he now stood. At that moment, he saw Jack step off the porch and get on a motor scooter.

Leonard pressed back against the fence. Suppose he came this way? Being spotted would ruin everything. He opened the gate and went inside the yard. If anyone's at home, he'd say he must have the wrong house. He heard the scooter start.

A second later it passed right by him.

~~~

"It's such a short notice," Jewel Banks fretted. "I don't even know if everyone's in town. What do you think, Ruby?"

Jack turned hopefully to Ruby. The three of them sat in the main salon of Jewel's boat.

"I'm game if you are," Ruby said.

Jack let out his breath. He hadn't called Jewel again about getting the band but instead had taken a chance on finding her at home. Ruby being there was a bonus.

"Suppose the others aren't available?" Jewel asked.

"I have my sax," Jack said. "We'll make it a trio."

"If you can borrow a keyboard, I can double on it and the guitar," Ruby added.

"This is going to be fun," Jack said excitedly. "How about we plan to start around eight?"

"Seven-thirty give us enough time to set up?" Ruby asked.

"Shouldn't be a problem,' Jack said. "And since you're big stars, I'll have a taxi pick you up here, say seven-fifteen."

"How should we dress?" Jewel asked.

"In whatever a Flamin' Flamingo and a Hot Jupiter would wear," Jack grinned.

Chapter 38

Dalton was in way over her head. She knew she should listen to Detective Bradshaw and stay out of Croaker's hair but now the events had taken another turn. This one more deadly.

She'd earlier gotten off the phone with Benny Spring's secretary. Talking to the woman had been inviting trouble, of course. But the credit card charges couldn't be ignored. She found out that a recent one had been made by a taxi in Miami. The amount suggested it wasn't just for a trip across town.

She had then called the cab company and learned that the fare was for a ride from Miami to Key West. She couldn't imagine anyone doing that without having an awfully good reason.

There was no longer time for decorum. Yeah, it was Hollywood's case. So what? She picked up her phone and punched in a 305 area code number.

Gleason had settled on the sofa in his apartment when his cell rang with *I shot the sheriff*. He didn't recognize the caller ID but answered anyway.

"This is Gleason," he said in his you're-under-arrest voice.

Dalton let out a breath before speaking.

"Hello Detective Gleason," she said. "This is Laura Dalton from Los Angeles. Do you remember me?"

Gleason sat up straight, disturbing the cat, who'd been sleeping on his lap.

"Laura. Of course I do."

"Sorry to bother you, Earl. But I have a slight problem and could use your help. It involves a mutual friend, Jack

Hunter."

Gleason laughed.

"No bother at all. I was just having a glass of wine with my cat. What do you need?"

"My apologies to the cat, then," Dalton laughed back. "First, do you know if Jack is still in Key West?"

"Oh, yes, he's here. In fact, he's been helping me on a case we're working. Though, 'helping' may not be quite the right word but you know how it goes with Hunter."

Dalton smiled to herself. She did indeed know.

"Here's the situation," she said.

Fifteen minutes later she'd finished briefing him, leaving out only one small detail—that she was in very hot water with her department.

"I'm sending you a picture of Leonard Hall," she said. "It's an intake photo from prison but he probably hasn't changed all that much."

"You have it there? Shoot it to me on my phone. I'll get it out to patrol. What do we do with this guy if we find him?"

"Hold him for credit card theft. But be careful, Earl. He may be armed."

Gleason sat up a little straighter at this.

"Does Hunter know he's out of prison?"

"No, I have to call him. What's he doing for you?"

Gleason went through the string of homeless homicides they were investigating.

"There's an off-chance that our friend might hear something at the soup kitchen," he said. "I don't have a lot of faith anything will come of it, though."

The idea of Jack snooping around to find a serial killer alarmed Dalton.

"Are you sure that's a good idea?" she said. "I mean, Jack's no baby but...isn't this kind of dangerous? I'd have thought you would have used undercover officers."

"He's only supposed to look, listen and report," Gleason

told her. "No heroics. Like I said, personally I don't expect it to be a big deal."

"With Jack it's never a big deal until it becomes one," Dalton said humorlessly.

Gleason let that lie.

"Think you'll be coming to Key West anytime soon?"

"I really don't have any plans at the present."

"Well, if you do, give me ring. I remember our dinner. Maybe we can do that again. Or the next time I'm on the Left Coast, I'll call you."

"That would be nice, Earl. I'll get that photo off to you now."

~~~

Leonard had waited until dark before setting out for Ashe Street. This time he cut over to Angela past the cemetery. As he approached the house, he saw there were lights on but no sign of the motor scooter. Could be parked around back. He checked the pistol he'd stuffed in his waistband and walked up to the front door and knocked loudly.

"Coming," a voice inside shouted.

Footsteps followed.

Leonard placed his hand on the gun. Jack was in for a big surprise, he thought, adding a grim smile.

"You'll wake up the whole neighborhood with that damn racket," Bobby Sunshine grumped, throwing back the door.

"I'm looking for Jack Hunter," he said, taking a moment to collect himself. He hadn't expected someone else to be there.

"Jack doesn't live here anymore," Bobby said, starting to close the door.

"He's due a settlement," Leonard said quickly. "Do you know where he lives now?"

"What kind of settlement?" Bobby asked suspiciously.

217

"A payment. From Los Angeles."

"That so?" Bobby said. Something about this bird bothered him. He called out to Derrick.

"Derrick, fellow here looking for Jack. You want to talk with him?"

Leonard took a step back as the doorway suddenly filled with a three-hundred pound giant.

"What's this about Jack?" Derrick said.

"It's a private matter. Just give me the address."

"You have a name and where you can be reached? I'll tell him."

"I need to see him now."

"You need to get some manners, sir."

Derrick shut the door in his face.

Leonard raised his fist to knock again but decided against it. He walked off the porch and stood on the sidewalk looking at the house. This was all so confusing and nothing like he'd planned. Who were these strange people and where was Jack Hunter? He headed back to his room to think.

~~~

Jack had brewed an espresso with his new coffeemaker and taken it out on the deck to enjoy with the morning paper. A nice article on the Inedible Cafe appeared on page three about how the restaurant had become a venue for local musicians. It included a photo of him holding his saxophone.

He'd given the interview a few days earlier. The reporter, however, had been at the restaurant last night and was able to add a review for the entertainment before the paper went to press. It also mentioned that Jack lived on a boat named the *Joyful Noise* in Key West Bight. Just to add a little interest.

It was certainly of interest to Leonard Hall, who also happened to be reading the newspaper at that moment.

~~~

"Detective Gleason, think I spotted that guy you're looking for," the patrol officer said, catching him in the hallway at the police station.

Gleason had earlier handed out flyers to the day watch he'd printed from the photo Dalton sent. He told the officers that the subject was wanted for questioning by the Los Angeles Police Department. That the LAPD had reason to believe he was now in Key West and as a courtesy, the KWPD would keep an eye out. And lastly, he cautioned that the individual may be armed.

"I was coming off watch and saw a man sleeping on a bench over by the Blue Bayou," the officer continued. "I rousted him, checked his ID, usual procedure. Had a California driver's license. Said he was a writer here for the convention and staying at the DoubleTree. Claimed he'd gone for a late night walk and fell asleep."

"Do you remember his name?" Gleason asked.

"Better, I wrote it down. I always do a field ID."

Gleason thanked the officer for his good work and checked his watch. LA should be awake by now.

~~~

"I need to stay another night," Leonard said.

"We can do that, Mr. Spring," Heather squeaked. "I just had a cancellation. Your room is available. Shall I just put it on the same card?"

"That's good. I might leave early tomorrow morning."

"Okay. I'll run it later today. Just drop the key in the jar when you go. So how do you like Key West?"

"It's improving."

~~~

"That must be an older picture," the desk clerk said. "He looks younger in it."

Three years in prison will do that, Gleason thought. He and Powers had driven to the DoubleTree with a copy of

219

Leonard's photo

"But you do remember him being here, is that right?" Gleason said.

"Oh, yes," the clerk nodded. "Not a very nice man. He came in late a couple of nights ago wanting a room. I told him the hotel was full but he didn't believe it. Made a scene."

"Was he alone or with someone?"

"Alone as far as I know."

"How did he arrive?" Gleason asked. "Private car, taxi, what?"

"Oh, that was funny. Like I said, the hotel is full with the writer's convention so I offered to call him a taxi. Maybe something was available in town. He huffed all up and told me he had a taxi waiting and then walked out. I didn't see any waiting in front. If there had been one, it'd long gone."

"And he didn't return?"

"Nope. Never saw him again. What'd he do?"

"Just need to talk with him. Thank you for your help."

The two detectives got in their car and headed back to the police station.

"Didn't patrol say he'd found this guy right about here, sir?" Powers asked, as they passed Garrison Bight. "There's a bench up ahead."

"Yeah, hell of a walk from the hotel. Good thing it wasn't during the middle of the day. He might've gotten heat stroke."

"So about this history Leonard Hall has with Jack Hunter," Powers said. "He murdered his wife?"

"That's my understanding. I haven't looked into the case myself. But a friend, actually a fellow officer with LAPD, was involved in the investigation."

Gleason had given Powers a fuller account than what he'd told patrol.

"She knows Hunter and believes he's at risk."

"California must have an amazingly liberal sentencing

law," Powers said.

"The judge screwed up at the trial. Wrong instructions to the jury."

"So now our buddy Jack Hunter faces double trouble," Powers said, biting her lower lip. "He's looking for one killer while another one is looking for him. Sounds pretty melodramatic. Does he know about this guy being in town, sir?"

"I would imagine Detective Dalton has warned him by now."

"Maybe we'd better give him a shout just to be safe, you think?"

Gleason shrugged.

"Fine by me. Call him after we get to the station."

"That photo. Did you notice there's a slight resemblance between that guy and Hunter? I mean, they could be long-lost cousins. Well, maybe fourth or fifth."

Gleason turned his head toward her.

"I'm sure he'd appreciate your pointing that out to him," he said.

Powers laughed.

"Just a crazy thought, that's all."

They drove on in silence until they arrived at the police station.

"I've been going through the murder books," Powers said, getting out of the car. "I've found something that might be interesting."

Chapter 39

She knew it. Would they listen now? Well, they'd better. Detective Bradshaw should be in any minute. She'd like another coffee but her stomach was too sour. Instead, she drummed her fingers nervously on the desktop in the detective's room.

Dalton had driven straight to Van Nuys after talking with Gleason, her mind racing at twice the speed limit down the 101 with questions. Would they pick up Leonard? Could they hold him? Suppose he got to Jack first?

And here? What proof does anyone really have that Leonard is responsible for Benny Spring's death? Circumstantial at best. That's exactly what her boss will say. What Moyer over at Hollywood will tell her. Even Croaker will agree, offering a smirk. Still, the chain of evidence, even indirect evidence, can link the person to the crime.

A couple of detectives came into the room to begin their day. Where the hell was Bradshaw? It was early.

She'd phoned Jack as soon as she had gotten off the line with Gleason but it went to message. She had to warn him. She should've done so earlier but she'd wanted to wait until she was certain. There'd only been conjecture on her part at the beginning. Then there was Lugo Croaker. Kibitzing at every turn. Lying. And she'd let her past with the man cloud her judgment. Now there was no denying that Leonard Hall was in Key West. She punched Jack's number again.

Tom Bradshaw walked in carrying a cup of coffee just as Jack's voice mail picked up. She left a quick message.

"I have some news about Leonard Hall," she said.

Bradshaw grunted, sat down at the desk and removed the top from his coffee.

"Let's hear it," he said, taking a sip.

She began with Benny Springs's credit card charges, the last one being the enormous taxi fare in Florida, and concluded with the fact she'd involved the Key West Police Department in the search for Leonard.

Bradshaw nodded and tightened his mouth.

"Has Mr. Hunter also been notified?" he asked.

"I haven't spoken with him directly."

"Well, let Key West handle that. You and I are taking a walk."

Neither one spoke until they'd gotten outside the building. Then Bradshaw turned to Dalton.

"Laura, there are guidelines," he said. "You've stepped all over them. And now this latest. You had no business contacting that woman about those credit charges. That's Hollywood's business. What do you think I should do about you?"

"Tom, I realize I may have been too aggressive but a life is at stake here. If I've overstepped my position, I can't help it. Croaker isn't doing a damn thing and someone might die because of it. You know what Spring's secretary told me? That Croaker called her for a copy of the credit statement. She said that she wanted to close the account but thought she needed a death certificate. He told her to keep the account open and don't worry about anything, he'd get back to her. He hasn't called her since."

"Maybe he's on top of it, Laura. In touch with the credit company himself. Knows all about those new charges."

"The only thing he's on top of is covering his ass. Leonard Hall has been ID'd in Key West. Does anyone care?"

"All right, Laura, we'll get to that. But first I want to know what it is with you and Detective Croaker before this goes any farther. Now."

Dalton hesitated for a moment, her eyes filling.

224

"Tom, can we just let it go that we went through Academy together, okay?"

~~~

All homicide investigations in every police department begin with a ring binder notebook into which a record of every single step of the investigation is entered. It's called the murder book and is kept current and open until the case is closed.

Powers had spread out the murder books on the table in the detective's room. She'd placed them in order of deaths, starting with Richard Kirby and ending with Wayne Teague.

She and Gleason were there alone.

"Each victim was murdered by a different means but all share a common element," she began. "Overkill."

"Yes, I believe we've already been over that," Gleason said.

"That's true, sir, but there's something else about them I hadn't noticed before."

She removed the gold charm from the evidence packet.

"This is the key."

She pointed at the first murder book.

"Kirby."

Then the next.

"Endress."

And down the line.

"Irwin...Teague. Put 'em all together and you almost spell *Keith*."

A smile creased Gleason's face was he began to see where she was heading.

"All that's missing is the *H*," she said, returning his smile." As for why anyone would do this, I go back to my old commanding officer. He said the reason for killing a person only has to make sense to the killer."

"This is right up there with reading tea leaves," Gleason

said, "but it's more than we had before."

"Yes, now we need to find Keith."

"But what about the shooter at Rest Beach?" Gleason asked. "Where does he fit?"

"I think he may have been a practice kill, sir."

Gleason shook his head.

"Okay. How many jewelry shops left on the list?"

"Just a couple."

"Probably our last shot on this. Better take it quick."

"Yes, sir. Also, shouldn't we check with KOTS? If there're any *H*'s registered, we need to warn them."

"Yeah, but I don't want to start a panic."

"Maybe we can narrow the list, sir. Some of the victims were known to deal. Drugs could be the thread."

"You could stitch up half the island with that," Gleason said. "Besides, these were petty dealers, if even that. Not something anyone would kill over. Especially using the amount of violence we've seen.'

"Then it's back to the charm," Powers said. "Who's Keith?"

~~~

Leonard came to the Key West Bight at the foot of William Street. He was starting to get onto the map and had lost his way only once. He walked through the parking lot to the docks, where he saw an armada of yachts spread across the horizon. This wasn't going to be easy.

"Help you with anything let me know," the shopkeeper asked.

He'd gone into a store to get out of the heat, which had risen above his acceptable limit though it was still early in the day.

"Maybe you can," he smiled. "How would I find a boat here?"

"Take your pick," she laughed, sweeping her hand toward the docks.

"No, I mean a particular one."

"If you know its name, the dock master can tell you where it's berthed."

~~~

Jack and Mike Galvin were finishing lunch at the soup kitchen. Today's special had been grilled cheese sandwiches and coleslaw.

"How're the new digs?" Mike Galvin asked. "Settled in?"

"Kind of nice," Jack said. "Different."

"Which part of town?"

"Key West Bight."

"No shit? You live on a boat?"

"Sort of a lend-lease deal," Jack said. "The owner loaned me the use of his boat since he and my landlady have moved into the house I was leasing."

"Big boat?"

"Big enough for me. Used to be a fishing boat. Been fixed up to cruise."

"Sounds great. What's its name?"

"Named after a church. Joyful Noise. Pretty wild, huh?"

"I wouldn't mind living on a boat," Galvin mused. "Just sail away whenever you want."

"I admit the idea has a certain appeal."

"Bet it did when you were homeless, Jack."

"Funny you should say that. I knew a great looking lady back then who lived on a sailboat and wanted me to sail away with her."

Galvin laughed.

"And you're still here? What happened?"

"Too much cocaine, I guess."

"Drugs, eh," Galvin said, eying him. "Didn't you tell me you never used them?"

The line at the serving window had about ended. A young man stepped up and held out his tray. Galvin placed a sandwich and cup of slaw on it.

"Hey, fellow," Galvin said brightly. "Haven't seen you here before. Where you from?"

The man shrugged and moved on.

"Always try to offer a friendly word," Galvin told Jack.

"Do you do that often?" Jack asked. "Strike up conversations with people who come through here?"

"Often? People who come through here? What is so fucking important about how *often* I talk to these people? Some law against that?"

Jack was startled by his sudden mood change.

"What the fuck's wrong with showing a little interest?" Galvin ranted, getting in his face. "Nobody gives a shit about them. You of all people ought to know that. Fuck!"

He removed his apron, tossed it on the counter and left the kitchen.

Jack couldn't understand Galvin's reaction. This might be something Gleason ought to know about. He took out his phone to call and found it had been turned off. And apparently for some time, he discovered when he turned it on, because he had ten messages waiting.

~~~

Detectives Tom Bradshaw and Bob Moyer had finished lunch at Musso & Frank on Hollywood Boulevard. Bradshaw had invited his counterpart to the famous restaurant, which serves the best martini in LA. Unfortunately, not for them today since they were both on duty.

"Van Nuys sure knows how to live" Moyer joked, taking in the surroundings while waiting for their to coffee arrive. "Hitting the Polo Lounge later?"

After Bradshaw had spoken with Dalton, he had looked into all of the evidence she'd compiled. Though she had gone outside of departmental policy and bulldozed her way into another jurisdiction, she hadn't broken any law. And to him what she had appeared to be solid. It was also clear that

Croaker wasn't doing his job. He had then called Moyer to set up the lunch. He'd particularly chosen a place more upscale, meaning pricey, than grabbing a bite at the favorite old Police Academy restaurant. He'd been right in that choice, too. There wasn't another cop in the joint.

"Thought you should see what you're missing," Bradshaw said. "Glad we got the chance to meet and talk."

"Same here. I still don't what the hell to make of all this, Tom."

"Well, there's no doubt Detective Dalton crossed a line," Bradshaw said. "Maybe two. But I don't believe any malfeasance was behind it. She's a good cop. One of the best I've worked with."

Moyer nodded.

"My problem is there's no proof of wrong doing by my d-two," he said. "Yeah, from what you've told me, he seems to be behind the curve on this case but maybe that's his style. Frankly, I haven't worked with the man all that long."

"What I'm thinking, Bob, is that we should keep this within our bailiwicks. There's no need for anyone filing a formal complaint and having it kicked upstairs. I've spoken with Laura and she's on board now. Hopefully, you could do the same with Detective Croaker. Everyone needs to take a time out. That doesn't mean dropping the investigation, however."

"I agree with you about Dalton being a good cop," Moyer said. "She impressed me that way. Probably why she stuck her nose in this investigation. But Croaker's making noises. Even hinting at sexual harassment."

Bradshaw hadn't mentioned to his counterpart about Croaker and Dalton going through academy together. While he felt there was obviously more to the story than just being classmates, at Dalton's request he hadn't pushed it any further. And he certainly wasn't going to bring it up here.

"I find that hard to believe, Bob. Laura Dalton's tough

and can be exasperating at times, but sexual harassment? No way she'd be involved in that kind of behavior. And isn't it usually the other way around?"

"Usually but not always."

"Well, you've got a point there. Still, that's just not in Dalton's makeup. Croaker's blowing smoke for some reason."

Bradshaw signaled for a refill on their coffee. A gruff male geriatric waiter, a hallmark of the restaurant, immediately brought over a pot.

"Like I said, he just recently came to Hollywood," Moyer continued. "Been kind of like musical chairs lately. My d-two recently retired on a disability. That was Mungers on the burglary table. He'd come over from Hollenbeck a few years ago. Croaker applied for the opening. Had a commendation for a gang bust in Southwest. Strikes me as the ambitious kind."

"That can be good and bad. Any other word on him from Southwest?"

"Rumor has it he's a lady's man," Moyer said. "Not necessarily in a good way."

Bradshaw made a mental note of that. Could something like that have happened between Croaker and Dalton?

"So what do you propose we do, Tom? I don't have a problem with keeping this in shop. I might have to toss Croaker a bone, though. Guess you'll also have to do something for your detective. Maybe not send her to Devonshire Division to work community relations?"

"I wouldn't wish that on a dog but how about this?" Bradshaw said. "Let's say Leonard Hall is involved with the Spring case. And let me add here that I believe Dalton is right about the security camera. She ought to know what he looks like since she worked the Ridenour homicide. I don't really know what the issue is between her and Croaker but airing any dirty laundry won't help. I suggest you and I form a task force of two and we liaison with the Key West detective. There's plenty of other work for Detective Dalton in Van Nuys and I imagine it's the same for your man in Hollywood."

Moyer considered that.

"So we take both of them off the Spring case and handle it ourselves," he said. "Okay, I'll go along with that."

"That's terrific, Bob. I was hoping you'd agree. What about the bone for Croaker?"

Moyer grinned.

"There's a celeb 187 in Hollywood that's sure to be taken away from us by Robbery Homicide any day now. I'll put Croaker on it."

Chapter 40

Leonard hadn't needed the dock master's help. He'd found the slip all on his own. He had noticed an odd-looking boat that stood out from the others berthed halfway down one of the piers. A closer look revealed its name. *Joyful Noise.*

Now he had settled on a bench off the boardwalk and where he could keep his eye on the boat. He had also bought a pair of cheap reflective sunglasses and a hat. There'd been no activity at the slip since he'd arrived. He noticed a man washing the deck of a larger yacht in the next one over. He got up and walked hurriedly to the pier.

"Good afternoon, sir," he greeted. "Trying to locate an old buddy who lives on a boat here. Told me its name but I forgot it. Something like that one next to yours."

"She just came in. Don't know who's on it. I haven't introduced myself."

"I'll come back later. Maybe surprise him."

~~~

Jack listened to all ten missed messages. Now he wished he'd never turned the phone on. He prioritized them and returned Laura's call. Her voice mail answered.

"Laura, this is Jack. My phone was off. I'll call Gleason. Thanks."

That was it. Leonard Hall had come to Key West, most likely intending to kill him, so he'd call Gleason, thank you. He shut off the phone again, got on his scooter and rode to Fort Zach.

Only a few people were at the beach and he had no trouble finding a quiet spot to himself. He settled on the warm sand and faced toward the Florida Straits. The band of green water at the shoreline quickly giving way to the darker blue of the depths. As always whenever he came to this spot, his thoughts were anxious to cross the ninety miles to Cuba. But this time he held them back. There were other matters to consider.

Laura had been very specific in her findings and he had no doubt that she was right. The only question he had was Leonard really that insane? Apparently so. The trial came to mind. Leonard's burning hatred toward him flaring up during it. Looks that could kill? Certainly. But here was the funny thing. He had felt the same about Leonard at the time. The only difference was he didn't show it then. Would he have gone through with it had he been given the chance?

Those feelings never left. He hadn't realized that until now. He was suddenly aware of a great weight having been lifted. A settlement long overdue now going to come to pass. He took out his phone and called Derrick Bean.

"Jack, haven't seen you lately. What's up?"

"Oh, this and that. Has anyone asked for me at the restaurant or the house? A stranger?"

"Yeah, some bloke came to the house. Nasty piece of work, in my opinion. Anyway we sent him packing. Hope he wasn't a friend."

Jack took in a breath.

"No, he isn't a friend. This is important. If that person shows up again, call the police."

"I can handle him, Jack."

"No, Derrick, you can't. Take my word."

~~~

Gleason gathered up the murder books and put them back in place. He'd continued to go over them after Powers had left the station. Now he was about to leave himself when the phone rang.

"Homicide. This is Detective Gleason."

"Detective Gleason, this is Detective Tom Bradshaw

with the Los Angeles department. How are you, sir?"

Gleason sat back down at his desk.

"I'm fine, detective. What can I do for you?"

Bradshaw explained the nature of his call and said that while they didn't have absolute proof that it was Leonard Hall who was using Benny Spring's credit card, they did have reason to suspect he might be and would appreciate any help Key West could give them.

"Detective Dalton believes it's Hall," Gleason said. "And one of our officers ID'd him as the man on the sheet she sent. He offered false ID but the officer didn't know that then. She's also concerned about her friend, Mr. Hunter."

"I understand that, detective. But even if it is Hall, there's no certainty he's there to harm anyone."

"I suppose that's a reasonable assumption. Key West *is* a tourist town. People are always coming down here for all sorts of reasons."

Bradshaw laughed.

"All right, all right, I know that sounded ridiculous. But I'm in the middle of a ticklish situation here. I won't go into that but if you do pick up the son-a-of-bitch, hold him for me. I've never been to Key West."

"Happy to assist, sir, and looking forward to showing you around town."

~~~

Heather sighed sympathetically.

"I know it must be some stupid mistake, Mr. Spring. Computers are always doing that."

Benny Spring's charge account had been closed.

"You'd already left when I ran the card. I'm sorry. Do you have another card we could use?"

This wasn't a surprise. Leonard had expected his luck to run out sooner or later. Just one more day would've been nicer.

"I don't have one. I'll pay cash. This is my last night anyway."

Heather sighed again.

Chapter 41

Jack had returned to the Bight and was now aboard the *Joyful Noise*. He'd called Gleason and Powers to tell them about Mike Galvin but both were gone for the day. He left a message with the desk.

Sunset celebrations had wound down at Mallory Square and shadows had begun to fill the harbor. It would soon be dark. Night always offered the advantage. He needed to be ready.

He assumed Leonard now knew where to find him. And he figured he'd probably come tonight. Whatever he had in mind, he would want to get it done quickly and leave.

Dalton had mentioned the missing gun in her phone message. He wondered if Leonard had ever used one. A gun. He'd never shown any interest in firearms when he had known him at the agency. He doubted if they gave lessons in prison. So his lack of knowledge, if true, could be another advantage.

He could lie in wait. Jump him when he set foot on the deck. A piece of pipe upside the head. Over and out. That'd be the smartest move but not the one he wanted.

He walked out of the cabin onto the deck.

"Hello, Jack," a voice called from the pier.

~~~

A bell announced Powers' entrance into the jewelry shop.

"May I help you, ma'am?" a small man standing behind the counter asked.

"I certainly hope so," she smiled, digging into her purse and removing her police ID. "I'm with the KWPD and we're trying to locate someone."

She removed the charm and handed it to the man.

"There's a name engraved on it. I realize this is pretty much a wild goose chase."

The man studied the gold disc for a moment and handed it back to her.

"Well, I don't know who 'Keith' might be," he said, "but I recently sold one of these with the same sentiment. He's apparently important to someone."

Powers took in a tiny breath. This was enormous.

"Do you remember who bought it?"

"Normally, I wouldn't. These are quite common and the engraving is ordinary. We sell a ton of them. But this individual was very memorable. He was a total asshole, if you'll pardon my French. Let me get my book."

He went to the rear of the store and returned with a ledger.

"Oh, yes," he said, running a finger down the page. "Here's the gentleman. Michael Galvin. Exasperatingly rude."

"You wouldn't have an address, would you?"

~~~

"Permission to come aboard," Mike Galvin joked.

"Sure, Mike, permission granted," Jack said.

Galvin threw a leg over the side and stepped onto the deck.

"This is pretty nice," he said, looking around. "Kind of different. I expected something more run-of-the-mill like one of these four or five million dollar babies parked along here."

"The neighborhood's changing. Do you live near the Bight?"

Jack couldn't imagine why Galvin had suddenly dropped in. He didn't even know the guy all that well. But it was the wrong time for a social visit. He had another matter pending. And besides, Galvin's mood changes made him uneasy.

"No, I live across town. Just was curious. Want to give me a tour?"

This was all Jack needed.

"Actually, someone's coming," he said. "Maybe another time?"

Galvin shrugged.

"Only take a minute, Jack. I really came to apologize for today. I was a jerk. Could we step inside? I've got a chill. Hope it's not one of those mosquitos."

Jack nodded and they went into the cabin. He left the door open.

"Boy, whoever built this knew what he was doing," Galvin said. "Look at that paneling."

"Get you a beer?" Jack asked, politeness overruling urgency.

"Don't want to put you to any trouble."

"None at all," Jack said, removing a bottle from the refrigerator.

"You joining me?"

"Got some business to attend to later," Jack smiled. "Need a clear head."

Galvin twisted off the top.

"Well, like I said, I'm sorry for being a horse's ass at the soup kitchen. You see, I also have business to finish. One letter left. One lousy letter and it keeps alluding me. You can't believe how frustrating that is. So near, so far, so near again. Enough to drive a fellow batshit crazy, huh?"

"I'm not sure I understand, Mike. What letter?"

Galvin's face clouded.

"It's not that difficult, Jack," he said, raising his voice. "We're not talking rocket science here. I need a fucking *h*. K-E-I-T-fucking H. Didn't you learn to spell in school? I thought you might be my *h* but now I'm not so sure. Tell me again about the drugs."

Jack's inner warning light flashed on high alert. He sized up Galvin. He figured he could probably take him in a fair fight. But there was seldom anything fair in a fight.

"There's nothing to tell, Mike. I don't use them. Never have. Why does that matter?"

Galvin laughed.

"You're shitting me, right? The girlfriend with the sailboat? All that coke?"

"Didn't happen, my friend. Wishful thinking on my part."

Jack's phone rang.

"I have to get this," he said, noting the caller ID.

Galvin shifted nervously on his feet.

"Where the hell are you?" Jack answered, stepping out the door and onto the deck. "Thought you were supposed to be here by now."

"I'm at home," Gleason said. "What are you talking about?"

"Yeah, all the way down C dock. I'm at the end. No, just a guy I work with. He's about to leave. See you in a minute."

"I have company coming," Jack told Galvin.

"Next time then," he said, hurrying past and clambering up the steps to the dock, shirttail flapping to reveal the buck knife sheathed in the small of his back.

~~~

Gleason was racing down Simonton in his car when his cell rang. He pushed the speaker button.

"Sir, this is Detective Powers. I have a name and address on the gold charm. Mike Galvin. Lives on Aubury. I'm heading there now."

"Hold off, Powers. I believe our man is with Jack Hunter. Come to the Key West Bight. The boat's at the end of C Dock. Some kind of fishing scow. I'm turning on Caroline Street right now."

He hung up and smoked the tires down Caroline to

Margaret and into the Lands End parking lot.

Though it was early night, the boardwalk still swarmed with tourists. Gleason pushed through a group and ran down the dock, careful to side-step the coils of rope and water hoses lying on the heavy wooden planks. Jack stood waiting on the deck of the *Joyful Noise*.

"You missed him by two or three minutes," he called out.

Gleason gulped a breath of air.

"Which way did he go?" he asked from the dock.

"Back the way you came. Might as well come down here so we don't have to shout."

Gleason boarded the boat.

"Powers is on the way," he said. "Tell me about this person, what's he look like?"

Jack described Galvin as best he could. Gave him a second rundown on what had taken place at the soup kitchen. Said he didn't know where he lived.

"Name's Mike Galvin, right?"

Jack nodded.

"Okay, I'm putting out a BOLO. Powers also has an address for someone with the same name. Could be your guy or not."

Gleason phoned in the be-on-the-lookout to KWPD and the Sheriffs. Powers arrived as soon as he'd finished.

"You have him in custody, sir?" she shouted from the dock.

"No, wait there. I'm coming up."

Then to Jack, "If Galvin is involved in any of these deaths, you're in danger. I'm going to leave an officer."

Jack didn't want any cops around. He was expecting another visitor.

"So he comes back and spots the cop and what?" he said. "He walks away, that's what. I appreciate your concern but a better idea is to let him return. He doesn't know it was you calling. I'll lock the door. Stall him until you can get back."

Gleason thought that over.

"I'd feel better leaving an officer," he said, "but you have a point. Okay, if he shows, call me. Try not to do something stupid."

Gleason gathered Powers and the two of them left for the Galvin address. Jack removed the table and chairs from the small deck and stashed them inside. He wanted the area clear for his next visitor.

It was almost midnight when Jack's cell rang and jolted him awake. He was sitting in the darkened cabin, a light burning in the forward sleeping area spilling through a porthole onto the dark water.

"Yeah?" he yawned into the phone.

"Gleason. You okay?"

"Slow night," Jack said. "Even the band at Schooner has quit."

"All right. Galvin's house is shut up, no one there. An unmarked will keep an eye out for the rest of the night. I'm heading home. Call me if you hear anything."

"Roger and out," Jack said with a small smile.

He got up and moved to a more uncomfortable bench-seat in the pilothouse. He looked across the harbor to the Coast Guard docks. Lights from the two cutters in port reflected undisturbed on the still black waters. Quietude settled over the Bight.

A muffled thump from outside startled him.

"Hey, your boat's sinking!" a voice yelled, followed by urgent knocking.

"I'm coming!" Jack yelled back and threw open the door.

"Hello, Jack," Leonard said. "Long time no see."

The light from a lamppost on the dock glinted off the Sig Sauer .40 he held pointed at Jack.

"Hello, Leonard. What brings you here?"

Jack stepped out of the doorway onto the deck. Leonard moved back.

"I've come to kill you, Jack."

"Really. You're the second person tonight."

A puzzled look crossed Leonard's face.

"That the gun you took from Benny Spring?" Jack asked, gesturing at the automatic.

Leonard didn't answer.

"LAPD's on your case, dummy," Jack said. "They know about Benny. You're going down for it. Remember Detective Dalton? She's been following your every move across the country. She's going to put your sorry ass back in jail."

"Too bad you won't be around," Leonard said.

"Suppose that's possible. But wait a minute, why would a tough guy like you need a gun? Or do you just beat up on defenseless women and old men."

Leonard laughed.

"Everything's a joke with you, isn't it?" he sneered. "I was a serious writer but you couldn't see it, could you? Neither could your whoring wife. She got what she deserved and now you're getting yours."

"You've got that wrong, Leonard. Then you're wrong about everything, aren't you? A serious writer? Now that *is* a joke. You're one deluded motherfucker, anyone ever tell you that?"

"Benny Spring didn't think so."

Jack smiled and shook his head.

"Benny was a Hollywood hustler. He ate chumps like you for breakfast."

"That's what you think," Leonard snapped. "He set a high bar."

"High bar?" Jack laughed. "His bar was so low it sat on the floor. Face it, you're a no-talent creep that people see through in a minute. That's what happened with Pamela, isn't it? She saw right through you. And you couldn't stand it. Benny did, too. Only he knew how to make a buck off cheap writing by punk wannabes like you. Hurt to hear that? Good. Fuck you. "

Leonard's eyes grew cold.

"You should've shown a little more respect back then, Jack. Maybe things would've turned out differently for everyone."

"Respect? Leonard, I've killed men I respected more than you," Jack said quietly.

Leonard brought up the gun and squeezed the trigger. Once. Twice.

"The safety's on, dip-shit," Jack said.

Leonard momentarily glanced down and Jack grabbed the gun. The two men stumbled backward together, Jack twisting Leonard's wrist and punching at him. The gun fired, the recoil jumping it from Leonard's hand and sending it skidding across the deck.

The sound of the report made Detective Gleason nearly spill his cold coffee. He'd been parked in the lot since leaving Jack.

Leonard brought his knee up hard between Jack's legs.

Jack went down and Leonard kicked at his head. But Jack covered himself, taking the blow on his shoulder. Leonard looked around for the gun, but not seeing it, scrambled to the dock and began running. Gleason appeared at the other end.

"Stop!" he yelled.

Leonard, not noticing a coil of rope lying at another berth, tripped and went flying headfirst into the water. The yacht's tie-off rope had formed in a slack loop above the surface and snagged him as he fell, snapping his neck as sure as a hangman's knot.

~~~

The coroner's van waited in the parking lot next to

Gleason's car. Leonard body had been fished out of the water and taken ashore, where it was about to be loaded onto a gurney.

"I thought it was Mike Galvin," Gleason said. "How are you feeling?"

He and Jack stood on the boardwalk by C Dock.

"Like I've been kicked in the nuts."

Gleason smiled.

"I meant about that," he said, motioning toward the van as the body was loaded inside.

"Glad it's over," Jack said.

The van's rear door slammed shut.

Chapter 42

Gleason walked into the detectives' room an hour later than usual the following morning. Powers was already there.

"Look like you could use a cup of coffee, sir."

A large cafe con leche waited on the desk.

"There're also some doughnuts," she added.

"Thanks, it was a pretty long night. Any news on Galvin?"

"Nothing yet. The house is still under surveillance. How is Mr. Hunter?"

"Lucky to be alive."

"Lucky that you decided to stick around in spite of him refusing protection. You should've called me, sir. I could have at least kept you company."

"No need for anyone to lose sleep over Jack Hunter," he laughed, checking his watch. "Wonder if Los Angeles is awake?"

~~~

Dalton pulled into the police parking lot and was getting out of her car when her phone rang. She recognized the caller number.

"This better be good, Jack. Do you know what time it is?"

She'd had a restless night and gotten up before daylight to come into the station.

"Leonard Hall is dead," he said.

Dalton sat back down in the car.

"Tell me what happened. First, are you okay?"

"I'm fine," Jack said and then spent the next five minutes running down the entire events of the night before.

"It's still difficult to imagine why he was so determined," Dalton said. "I can almost understand what happened between him and Benny Spring but why take off across the country to find you?"

"Insanity."

"I guess."

"The cops here have the gun and Benny's billfold. Gleason will probably call. Do you know if Leonard had any family or relatives? He never talked about it at the agency."

Dalton sighed. No matter the crime, there was always a family on both sides.

"I really don't know, Jack. I'm sure someone will claim the body."

"Gleason can handle that, too."

"Thanks for calling me, Jack. Take care."

After hanging up, she sat in the car for awhile.

~~~

"Sir, the Sheriffs picked up Galvin," Powers shouted, her hand over the phone.

Gleason was returning from the men's room.

"Tell them we're on our way," Gleason said.

The two detectives drove to the Sheriff's station on Stock Island where Mike Galvin was released to their custody. No words were exchanged between anyone on the ride back. Now the three of them were seated in an interview room.

"Comfortable, Mr. Galvin?" Powers asked. "Coffee, water?"

Galvin shook his head no, fingering the string around his neck.

"Detective Gleason and I are investigating a crime that hopefully you might have some information on," she smiled.

Gleason had given her the lead in the interview. Lt. Halderman sat outside watching the proceedings on closed circuit TV.

"First, I have something I'd like to show you," she said,

removing the charm from an envelope and placing it on the table. "Familiar?"

Galvin stared at the gold disc.

"There's an inscription," Powers said, picking it up, "Thank you. Keith. Does that help jog a few brain cells?"

Galvin unconsciously pulled out the string with the charm.

"May I see that?" Powers asked, holding out her hand.

He hesitated and then obediently gave it to her. She held both charms side by side.

"They exactly match."

"It's not an unusual piece," Galvin said. "Stores sell a ton. Could've come from anywhere."

"Possibly. But both having the same inscription? That's a remarkable coincidence."

"Coincidence happens," Galvin shrugged.

"The store where the charm you're wearing was bought is located on Duval Street. The jeweler remembered you, Mr. Galvin. Said you were very particular that the engraving match one you said you'd lost. Well, he didn't put it quite as nicely as that but it looks like you knew what you wanted. And I'd say he did a pretty good job, wouldn't you?"

Galvin laughed.

"Poor man said you nearly drove him crazy," Powers said. "In fact, you even insisted that he include a scratch that'd been on the original. And, lo and behold, here it is, right across the back just as you directed. You can't tell the two of them apart. Boy, that's some attention to detail, Mr. Galvin. I'm impressed."

"The jeweler's wrong," Galvin said. "I've always had that charm. Like I said, coincidence happens"

"I'm afraid it was you who made the recent purchase, sir. The store has a camera. You're on it."

Galvin shifted in his seat.

"So I stopped in the stupid store," he said. "Didn't see

249

anything I wanted and left."

"The date on the camera is the same one on the sales slip. The slip lists the purchase and engraving instructions and your name."

Halderman, sitting outside, slapped his thighs and grinned.

"All right, so I bought the charm. It was a replacement. I was embarrassed that I'd lost the original."

"That was a lot of trouble to go through? Couldn't you have just told Keith you'd lost it? I'm sure he would have understood. I certainly would."

"If he'd been alive maybe," Galvin said angrily. "Unfortunately, he's not thanks to the drug pushers."

"I've sorry to learn that. What was Keith to you? He must have been important."

"Keith was my brother. He had issues. I took care of him."

"So he gave you the charm for your help then, as a token of his appreciation. I can only imagine how much that meant to both of you. Do you remember where you lost it, Mr. Galvin?"

"No, it was just missing one day."

Gleason folded his arms. Galvin had just confirmed the charm they'd found at the murder scene belonged to him.

"His rights!" Halderman said aloud outside. "Read him his damn rights!"

Gleason stood up.

"Mr. Galvin, I believe we should read you your rights at this point," he said.

When Gleason had finished, Powers resumed the interview.

"That must have been painful," she said, pointing to a scar on his neck. "How'd it happen?"

"Don't remember."

"You don't? Yet you remembered amazing details about the charm. Almost photographically. I think you *do* remember how you were injured and where you lost the

250

charm. Further, I believe they occurred at the same time in the same place."

She reached into a folder and removed a stack of photographs.

"You may find these pictures shocking, Mr. Galvin. They were taken of homicide victims."

She began laying them out on the table top.

"This was Richard Kirby," she said. "Stabbed four times, throat slashed."

Galvin turned his head aside.

"I would appreciate your looking at them, sir," she said sternly. "Next Scott Endress. Brutally bludgeoned to death. Janice Irwin, horribly poisoned."

"And finally Wayne Teague. Throttled to death and badly beaten."

She paused to take a breath.

"That murder took place at the bridge. Where you lost the charm. This very one. And where you returned to search for it. Only it was no longer there. We found it."

Another pause.

"Four people viciously murdered with absolute malice," she continued. "All of them homeless. Why?"

She picked up the charm.

"I think the answer is here."

Galvin sat passively.

"Keith. K...E...I...T...," she read. "K for Kirby. E for Endress. I for Irwin. T for Teague. Only the H is lacking. Coincidence again, Mr. Galvin?"

"The one that got away," Galvin singsonged softly.

Gleason rose from his seat.

"Stand up," he ordered. "You're under arrest on suspicion of murder."

"I'm not a serial killer," Galvin shouted as Gleason cuffed him.

Chapter 43

Jack hadn't felt like spending another night on the boat after the encounters with both Mike Galvin and Leonard Hall. He'd gathered up a few things the next day, as if he were going away for a weekend, and had taken a room at the Pier House. It'd been nearly a month now.

"Another story about the Blue Bayou," Billy said, laying aside the daily paper. "People finally paying some attention to what goes on out there."

He and Jack were having coffee at the Inedible Cafe. This had become a routine every morning since he'd moved. Jack would stick around there until noon and then disappear for the rest of the day. Billy was worried about his friend but so far had kept it to himself.

"Maybe some good will come of it," Jack said.

"Wonder what's going to happen to the fellow did all those terrible things?"

"You mean Mike Galvin? My guess is they'll put him away forever. Gleason told me the other night at Vinos they have evidence that ties him to at least three murders."

Jack had been splitting his evenings between the Chart Room and Vinos. Another cause for concern to Billy.

"Be looking for somebody else at the soup kitchen, I suppose," he said. "You planning on going back?"

Jack smiled. He hadn't volunteered there since Galvin's arrest.

"Don't know, Billy. Might be just another star on my resume."

Billy got up from the table and went into the kitchen.

"Want to run something past you," he said, returning with a coffeepot. "Your giving your time helping to feed those folks got me to thinking. A lot of waste goes on here and at Stella by Starlight. Always throwing out good food at the end of the day. Maybe those people out there could use it."

Jack's attention perked up.

"What do you have in mind, Billy?"

"Well, there's always plenty of calamari that hasn't been cooked after calamari night. Order too much, hee-hee. And lately Derrick seems to have a fish or two he doesn't know what to do with when they close, so the fish go home with him. We could give all that to the soup kitchen. Maybe I could scare up a few other things, too. What do you think, Jack?"

This was a change of heart, Jack thought. Billy hadn't appeared all that sympathetic to the homeless before. He was genuinely touched. But then he realized he shouldn't have been surprised. Billy had always been a generous soul.

"That's a terrific idea," he said. "And I'll start a fund to cover the 'other things', including those wayward fish."

Billy smiled.

"About the other fellow, Jack," he said hesitatingly, "...the one that fell off the dock, I didn't know what he'd done to your wife until it was in the newspaper. You doing okay? Was afraid to ask before."

Jack shrugged.

"That happened a long time ago and yeah, it was a bad time for me. Then. People talk about closure like it's a damn door. Me? I just feel relieved. Pamela will always be here in my heart and mind. Gleason said he'd spoken with a couple of detectives in Los Angeles. They believe Hall murdered a man in LA before coming here. But since he's dead himself now, the District Attorney can't make a case. The poor guy the bastard killed is an unclassified death. Probably will always be. Isn't that something?"

"Don't make sense," Billy said. "How's that lady

detective friend of yours?"

"She's still a detective. We're still friends."

"I liked her. Hope she comes to see us again."

Jack nodded.

"Don't know what your plans are for that boat, Jack, but I just wanted to let you know there's a nice house for sale in Bahama Village."

"Thanks, Billy. I don't know what they are, either, but I'll keep it in mind."

"Just saying, that's all," Billy smiled.

"Bobby Sunshine is moving the boat back to Stock Island. I'm going to help him. Might be away for a few days."

"Take all the time you need, Jack."

~~~

The Florida Straits stretched in an unending blue line before him. How many times had he taken in this view lying on the warm sand at Fort Zach? Straining his eyes to look beyond the horizon and on to Cuba.

"Steer her zero-eight-seven, Jack," Bobby Sunshine said, standing next to him in the pilot house. "We'll run with the current some before turning south to Havana."

The *Joyful Noise* rose on a swell as Jack helmed her to a new course.

Thank you for reading.
Please review this book. Reviews help others find Absolutely Amazing eBooks and inspire us to keep providing these marvelous tales.

If you would like to be put on our email list to receive updates on new releases, contests, and promotions, please go to AbsolutelyAmazingEbooks.com and sign up.

Meet the Author

Robert Coburn has worked at major advertising agencies in New York and Los Angeles. His ads have won top awards both nationally and internationally. He is an instrument rated commercial pilot and plays saxophone. He and his wife now live in Carmel, California.

ABSOLUTELY AMAZING eBOOKS

AbsolutelyAmazingEbooks.com
or AA-eBooks.com

www.ingramcontent.com/pod-product-compliance
Lightning Source LLC
Chambersburg PA
CBHW070452030726
47503CB00004B/1011